When I woke up this morning, I was a lizard. I realized something was wrong the moment I rolled out of bed. The frame of the bed broke under my weight. I jumped as the mattress crashed to the floor, but I jumped too high, cracking my head on the ceiling and cracking the ceiling with my head. At the same time, my tail lashed the wall, knocking a large hole next to the window and spreading a shower of plaster. That made me sneeze, and I blew another hole in the wall.

"Hey, what's going on up there?" Dad shouted from below.

"Nothing," I tried to say. But it came out "Arrrrannnggg." This situation definitely had possibilities.

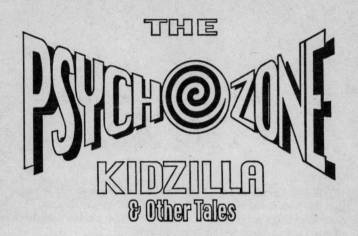

# THE PSYCHO ZONE

## KIDZILLA
### & Other Tales

# David Lubar

**Tor Kids!**

A TOM DOHERTY ASSOCIATES BOOK
NEW YORK

**For Mom, who always had time
for a trip to the library**

THE PSYCHOZONE: KIDZILLA & OTHER TALES

Copyright © 1996 by David Lubar

A Tor Book
Published by Tom Doherty Associates, Inc.
175 Fifth Avenue
New York, NY 10010

Tor® is a registered trademark of Tom Doherty Associates, Inc.

ISBN: 0-812-55880-4

First edition: April 1997

Printed in the United States of America

0  9  8  7  6  5  4  3  2  1

Reprinted by arrangement with Tom Doherty Associates, Inc.

# CONTENTS

# FAIRY IN A JAR

**Y**ou probably think of fairies, if you think of them at all, as wonderful little creatures flying happily through the forest, dancing and singing and making merry. Let me tell you something: Fairies might look lovely on the outside, but inside they are ugly, real ugly. Fairies are mean and vicious. They've got teeth like tiny needles. One bite wouldn't hurt much. But I'm pretty sure they wouldn't stop at one; they'd keep biting and chewing until they hit something vital. Fairies aren't good news. I know. Let me tell you about my fairy in a jar.

I'd been running around the backyard trying to catch fireflies with the net from this bug kit I'd gotten years ago. The kit was a birthday present from an aunt who had no idea what I liked. I might have used it once or twice, but mostly it just sat at the back of my closet under a pile of other junk. I'd lost the collecting bottle that came with it, but I found an old jar and punched a couple of holes in the lid. Bugs probably didn't need much air, but it was fun banging away with a hammer and nail. Anyhow, I was swiping the net at some bugs because there was nothing on TV except reruns and all my friends were busy and I couldn't find anything else to do.

I'd caught a couple fireflies and put them in the jar. The whole adventure was getting boring pretty fast. I was just about to quit when I saw a flash under the birch tree at the back of the yard near the woods. Thinking about it later, I sort of remember that the flash was different. It was more glittery, almost a sparkle.

I crept over and swung the net.

*Thunk!* Something heavy hit the bottom. I jumped. I thought I'd caught a bat. My skin crawled at that idea. I fumbled the jar lid open and slammed the net down. I felt a solid plunk against the glass. *Got it,* I thought. I needed two tries to get the lid on right. The jar kept shaking in my hand. So did the lid.

A bat. My very own bat. The guys would go wild when I showed it to them.

I held the jar up to see my catch. Three fireflies were crawling around the sides. But that wasn't what grabbed my attention. There was something else crumpled on the bottom. It wasn't a bat—not even close. It wasn't an *it*, either. It was a she.

She unfolded herself and rose slowly to her feet, shimmering in the light of the quarter moon. She was no more than five inches tall. Skinny. Long dark hair. Green dress. Wings. She looked down at her body, as if checking for injuries. The jar was still shaking in short jerks that made her stagger and fight for balance. She pressed her hands against the glass and stared straight at me. For an instant, so quick I thought at first it was my imagination, there was nothing in her gaze but pure hatred.

Then she smiled.

Maybe I should have smashed the jar against the tree. Maybe I should have smashed it and run—just run and run forever. "Maybe" isn't worth much—it's only a word. In a way, I understood how that kid at the playground must have felt last week when I punched him in the gut. Everything inside of me was stunned. I felt that my body had been filled with glue. I held the jar and stared at her.

*"Let me go, kind sir."* Her voice was like bells and dreams and whispers in my mind.

I grabbed the lid. I started to twist it loose, but that look of hate flashed across her face again. I knew. In that thousandth of a second, I knew I could never set her free. By then, I also knew I didn't want to set her free. She was mine. I had captured a prize no one else could even imagine.

◀ 3 ▶

*"Wishes,"* she said. *"I can grant wishes."*

That got my interest. I took my hand off the lid and held it out, palm up. "Show me. A thousand dollars. Right here." I wiggled my fingers.

*"You have to free me first."*

"I don't think so." I wasn't stupid. I wasn't going to fall for some sort of trick.

*"That is the rule."* Her voice grew colder.

"I make the rules now." It felt good to say that.

*"Please."*

"No."

Still staring at me, she flicked her hand out and grabbed one of the fireflies from the side of the jar.

Still staring at me, she raised the struggling insect to her mouth.

Still staring, she bit off the head of the firefly.

I don't know if she kept staring after that. I looked away. But I squeezed the jar, as if to make sure the glass was strong enough to keep her trapped. It was one of those jars people put home-made stuff in. The lady next door had this wormy old apple tree. Each year she made applesauce for the whole neighborhood. Every house got a jar, tied with a red ribbon. No one ever eats it. We just toss out the whole thing, or dump the sauce and keep the jar. The glass felt solid. It would hold her.

I took the jar up to my room, being careful that nobody saw it. I put it on the top shelf in my closet.

The next morning, I almost convinced myself

none of it had happened. Almost. But the jar was there. And she was there. At first I thought she was dead. She was crumpled on the bottom again. Then, as I saw her let out a shallow breath, I realized she was sleeping—sleeping or in some sort of suspended state. *Creature of the night.* I don't know where that phrase came from, but it ran through my head. I noticed something else. The bugs were gone—all three of them. *Bon appetit.*

I shook the jar a bit, but she just slid around without waking. I could wait. She'd be up after dark. I was pretty sure of that. Somehow, some way, I was going to get a payoff from her.

Sure enough, when I checked that night, she was awake, sitting on the bottom of the jar. "Good evening," I said, speaking quietly so nobody would hear me talking in my room.

*"Set me free. I shall reward you with wonders beyond your imagining."* She looked up at me and smiled. A chill ran down my spine.

"Cut the babble and give me some details. What can you do?" I picked up the jar, holding the sides of the lid. Even protected by the glass, I didn't want to put my fingers too close to her.

*"Whatever you wish."*

I didn't believe her. Promises were easy to make. "Show me."

*"Free me first."*

I shook my head. It was a standoff, but I was the one with the power. She was mine. She would give me something valuable. She had no choice. I owned her now. "Think about it," I said, putting the jar back on the shelf. "Think of some way to buy your freedom. I'm sure you'll come up with an idea."

She gave me that look again, and a flash of those teeth. I closed the closet door and left the room. The next day, we had the same conversation, and the same again on the day after. I wanted proof. She wanted freedom. But she was weakening. I could see that. I knew she had to give me a reward sooner or later. I could wait. I was in charge.

On the fifth day, she agreed to my request. *"I will transmute an object for you,"* she said. Her voice was thinner, barely louder than a thought.

"Transmute?"

*"I will change its form. Give me carbon. I will make a diamond."*

"A diamond? That's more like it." I wondered for a moment how I was going to sell a diamond. But that problem could wait. Right now, I needed some carbon. That was easy enough. Charcoal for the grill, that was carbon. So was the graphite in pencils. So were diamonds. They were all just different forms of carbon. I couldn't believe that something I learned in Mr. Chublie's stupid science class was actually worth knowing. Live and learn. But I wasn't about to try to stick a big hunk of charcoal in the jar. There was no way I was opening that lid, not even for a second. I wasn't falling for any of her tricks. As I looked around the room, I saw the answer right next to me.

I yanked out my desk drawer and hunted around the sides and corners. "Got it." Perfect. I knew I had it in there—a whole pack of refills for my mechanical pencil. The best part was that they were thin enough to slip through the airholes in the lid of the jar. I was planning to keep a nice, solid barrier between me and those teeth, thank you.

She gathered the pieces of lead. *"This will take some time."*

"I can wait."

She sat staring at the slivers of carbon. I put the jar away for the night. In the morning, I rushed to the closet to see my first diamond. In my head, I'd already spent the money—a new bike, new sneakers, all the new video games. The guys were definitely going to envy me.

But she wasn't finished. The pieces of lead were still there, though they looked smaller and shinier than before. *"It takes time,"* she said.

I would have to be patient.

*"It takes time,"* she warned again that evening.

I waited. On the fourth night, she was done. *"Here."* She held up her hand. *"Take this and set me free."*

"What are you trying to pull?" I almost smashed the jar. There was nothing more than the tiniest sparkle in her tiny hand. She had made a miniature diamond chip. It was worthless. My dreams of wealth turned pale and vanished.

*"This is all I can give you. Take it and set me free. You made a bargain."*

I was so disgusted, I just put the jar back in the closet and went to bed. Maybe I heard something that night. I can't remember. I'm too scared to really remember. But I remember the morning. Every second is burned into my brain.

I got up. I walked to the closet. The door was open about an inch. I'd thought I'd closed it. I opened it all the way and reached for the jar. My hand stopped. My breath stopped. My heart almost stopped. There was a hole in the side of the jar. There was a round piece of glass on the shelf next to the jar. She was gone.

*How?* Then I knew. The diamond. She'd tricked me. She knew I wouldn't take that tiny diamond. She also knew it could cut through the glass.

She was free. Somewhere, she was sleeping. But night was coming. And she would wake. And she would come for me.

I'm afraid to go to sleep tonight. I don't think I will ever sleep again.

# THE TOUCH

Laura thought a flea market would be fun. It sounded wonderful. "There'll be all kinds of things to see," her mom had said. "You'll love it."

But it was just a bunch of junk—nothing but a lot of people sitting around in the hot sun trying to sell things that nobody wanted. It was boring. The buyers looked bored. The sellers looked bored. Even the stuff being sold looked bored. And every five seconds her mom would warn her "Don't touch" or "Look with your eyes, not your hands, Laura."

Right. Like she really wanted to touch any of that junk. She'd have to wash her hands for a week to get them clean after putting her fingers on any of this stuff. Laura looked at the table in front of her. There was a box of moldy books— the same books everyone else was selling. There was another box with record albums. *Records,* Laura thought. *Who in the world would want those ancient things?* There was a ratty old doll with a stained dress and a chip missing from her cheek. Her hair was tangled and stiff. *Yuk,* Laura thought.

"Mom, can we go now? Pleeeeeaaase."

"In a minute," her mom muttered. She was studying an old butter dish like it was the lost treasure of ancient Egypt.

Sure. Laura knew what "in a minute" meant. She was doomed. She searched the table again, desperately hoping to see something that would hold her interest for a moment or two. She glanced at the woman in the folding chair behind the table. She must have been ninety years old. She was sitting there, staring off to one side, paying no attention to the items she'd set out for sale.

Laura shivered and looked back at the table. Dancing light sparkled in the sun as Laura moved her head. Her eyes were treated to a flash of red, followed by rainbow bursts. Laura gasped. Right in front of her, nearly lost among the rusty tools and cracked dishes and rotted magazines, was the most beautiful, unexpected treasure.

Could it be? Laura stepped closer, pressing against the edge of the table. Her hand darted out, then stopped halfway. She glanced to the left. Her mom had put down the butter dish and was examining a tarnished fork. Laura gazed back toward the crystal horse. It was the most lovely thing she had ever seen. The sight brought back memories of a merry-go-round she had ridden long ago. Every detail was carved in this ornament—the flying mane, the ribbon-covered pole, the fancy saddle. Laura could almost hear the music and feel the rise and fall of the horse as they rode in circles on a summer day.

She glanced around again. Her mom wasn't looking. The old lady wasn't looking. Laura had to touch that sparkling crystal treasure. It was calling her. She reached out to pick it up. She lifted it.

She felt a snap.

A leg broke. It fell with a small tinkle to the table. Laura froze. She waited for the shouting. There was nothing. The flea market buzzed on around her as if she hadn't just destroyed the most beautiful jewel in the world. Trying not to attract attention, Laura lowered the crystal horse to the table. It started to fall as she put it down, tilting toward where the leg had been. She leaned it against the side of the doll with the chipped cheek.

"Mom, can we go?"

Her mother sighed. "All right, but don't ask me to bring you here again."

*No problem,* Laura thought as she moved from

the table. She hurried away, but a burning feeling in the back of her neck made her spin around. Behind her, the woman slowly turned her head toward Laura. She looked right at her. She looked right *through* her. The woman raised her left hand. She touched her left palm with her right forefinger. Laura watched, not understanding, wanting to explain that it wasn't her fault.

The woman flung her arms apart. Laura jumped. The woman laughed, then whispered several words.

Laura's fingers tingled. She glanced toward the horse. It wasn't there. The woman's laugh echoed in her head. Laura fled to her mom.

That night, when she went to bed, Laura was sure she was going to have nightmares about the flea market. "Sweet dreams," her mom said as she turned out the light. Laura waited until her mom left the room. Then, feeling just a bit childish, she rushed to her closet and hunted for Mister Hoppy. In the dim glow of the light from the hallway, she searched for the stuffed animal that she had slept with when she was little. It was silly, but she knew she needed Mister Hoppy tonight.

"There you are," she said when she spotted the stuffed rabbit with the bright blue eyes and floppy ears. As she picked it up, her hand tingled for a second.

She had no dreams that night.

When she woke the next morning, the flea market itself seemed almost a dream. Feeling foolish about her fears, Laura reached to put Mister Hoppy back in the closet.

"What the . . . ?" She couldn't find the bunny. It must have fallen to the floor. She looked. It wasn't on the floor. It wasn't under the bed or tangled in the sheets. It was just gone.

*It has to be here somewhere,* Laura thought. She knew she'd find it later.

Laura went down the stairs and into the kitchen. A wonderful smell greeted her. "Waffles," she said when she saw what her mom was making. "My favorite."

"Just in time for breakfast, sleepyhead," her mom said. "I was getting ready to wake you."

Laura grabbed a plate from the cabinet and went over to the counter. "There you go," her mom said, lifting the hot, crispy treat out of the waffle iron. "By the way, I'm expecting an important call this morning, so don't tie up the phone."

"Yes, Mom." Laura carried her breakfast to the table. The waffle looked perfect. She could already imagine how fabulous it would taste. As she set the plate down, the waffle started to slide off. She stopped it with her free hand. There was a small tingle in her fingers. Laura let go of the plate and went to get the syrup.

"My word," her mom said. "You really wolfed that one down. You must have been starving. Would you like another?"

"What?" Laura was puzzled by the question.

She walked back across the room and looked down at her plate. It was empty.

"Would you like another waffle?" her mom asked again.

Laura nodded. *This can't be happening,* she thought. She touched the plate and waited for the tingle. Nothing. She touched the table. Nothing. She thought about Mister Hoppy. Had he vanished like the waffle? *Did it only happen to important things?* Laura had to find out. She needed to touch something she cared about. She jumped from her seat. The chair crashed over as she ran to the living room.

"Laura!" her mom called after her.

*What can I try?* Laura wondered. There, on the table—the book she was reading. It was her favorite series. She touched it. Nothing—no tingle. She ran to the playroom. She started grabbing, touching, feeling—new toys, old toys. Nothing.

"Laura!" Her mom gripped her shoulder and spun her around. "What is it? What's wrong?"

Laura clutched her mother's hand, wondering how she could possibly explain. "Mom—" She stopped. There was a tingle.

"What is it?"

Laura was afraid to look away. She knew what would happen the second she took her eyes off her mother.

The phone rang.

"Stay there. I'll be right back." Her mother pulled free of Laura's grip and dashed from the room.

"Wait!" Laura shouted as she rushed after her. She stumbled over one of the toys she'd dropped. She caught her balance and raced toward the doorway.

"Mom!" Laura called.

The phone kept ringing in the kitchen. It rang and rang, unanswered. The ringing filled the room ahead of her.

Laura burst into the kitchen. There was no one there. She was alone.

Laura curled into a ball and grabbed her head in both hands and screamed. And through her screams, through the pounding fear that seized her mind and the shaking tremors that tore through every muscle of her body, she felt a tingle in her fingers where they touched her face.

The ringing stopped.

# AT THE WRIST

**I**t wasn't my fault that Dad cut his hand off. I can't take any of the blame for that. Okay, I was in the room at the time, but I didn't do anything to startle him. He cut his hand off all by himself. As he would have said if I had done it, that was one bonehead move, one really stupid stunt.

He sort of messed up the workshop, too. But Dad probably won't be doing much woodworking in the future, and I certainly don't have any urge to tangle with power tools. I think some of them try to get you.

Okay, I guess I've made the point that none of it was my fault. At least, not Dad's accident. But then I had an accident of my own. When the guys from the ambulance came, they rushed away with Dad as fast as they could. Right after they left, I noticed that they'd forgotten to take his hand. I knew that the doctors could put it back on. Doctors do that kind of stuff on television all the time. It's called microsurgery. It's no big deal.

So I got some ice from the freezer and put it in the little cooler—the one Dad fills with soda when he's going out to a ball game. I got a bag from the drawer and grabbed the hand through the plastic. It felt kind of weird, like taking a steak out of the refrigerator, except it wasn't cold. Trying not to think about what I was doing, I picked up the hand and put it in the cooler. Then I put in more ice. As I was shutting the lid, the phone rang. I ran to the living room and answered the call. It was my friend Carl. I told him I didn't have time to talk. I hung up the phone and went back to the kitchen. The cooler had popped open, so I shut the lid again. Then I jumped on my bike and pedaled to the hospital.

But somewhere along the way, between the time I picked up the hand and the time I got to the hospital, I must have messed up. When the nurse opened the cooler, there was nothing in it except for the ice.

I'd lost Dad's hand.

This was not good. I went back to the house. On the way, I looked over the whole route I'd taken, hoping to spot the hand. No sign of it. I searched the house. Not a trace. Mom came back from the hospital and started looking. Even the cat sort of helped to look. At least, he sniffed around a lot. None of it did any good. We all came up empty handed.

"Well, where did you have it last?" Mom asked.

*If I knew that, it wouldn't be lost,* I thought, but I didn't say anything. I figured I was in enough trouble already. That wasn't really fair since I'd been trying to do a good deed.

As hard as we looked, we couldn't find the hand. After a few hours, it became a dead issue, to use a rather sick phrase. They can only sew stuff back if it's still in good condition. A hand doesn't keep very well if it isn't cold.

Dad came home two days later, but he didn't speak to me very much. I guess he was angry about his hand getting lost, but I don't see how it could have been my fault.

Another week passed. That's when it started. I was falling asleep, just drifting, not really asleep yet but definitely close. All of a sudden, out of nowhere, WHACK! Something smacked me on the butt so hard I thought my head would pop off.

I sat up fast, one hand reaching down to rub my stinging flesh. There was nobody in the room.

I thought I heard a faint scurrying, like someone scratching at a rug. But I wasn't listening very carefully. I was too busy trying to ignore the pain in my rear. It felt like I'd been hit by the world's champion of butt-smacking.

I looked around the table at breakfast the next

morning, suspecting everyone but knowing that nobody there could have done it. Dad was still pretty weak. Mom was no powerhouse. My brother Ed was a runt, and my sister Darlene was only three. She could have hit me with all her strength and I might not have noticed.

"Something wrong?" Mom asked when she caught me staring.

"Nope," I lied. "Everything is fine."

"Fine for you," Dad muttered as he tried to butter a piece of toast. He'd been making a lot of comments like that the last few days. I half expected him to take me to the woods any time now and leave me stranded, or drown me in a sack in the lake like an unwanted kitten.

Nope, I decided it wasn't any of them. I was beginning to think that I'd imagined the whole thing. I'd been almost asleep. And there was no bruise or anything. I hadn't checked until morning, and it's not all that easy looking at your own butt in a mirror, but there certainly was no sign that anything had actually smacked me.

Real or not, it happened again the next night. This time, I was asleep. At least, I was asleep until I felt the smack. It was quickly followed by a second whack. I rolled over and sat up fast.

There was no one in the room.

I held my breath and listened for the scurrying sound. There was definitely something crawling across the room and scrabbling out the door. It was fast. In a moment, it had reached the hallway.

Then the sound changed as the thing moved over the wooden floorboards.

I think, when I heard the sound of fingernails on wood, I began to suspect what I was dealing with. But I didn't want to face that possibility. I just didn't want to believe that Dad's hand had come back to punish me.

Nothing happened that night. But, two days later, after taking a couple of hard swipes on the rump, I almost managed to catch hold of it. For an instant, our fingers met. There was no doubt. It was a hand. I couldn't identify it for sure as Dad's hand, though it was definitely big and kind of hairy. I doubted there were other hands out there itching with an urge to smack me.

Two thoughts crossed my mind. First, I had to do something to stop this or I'd end up spending the rest of my life avoiding hard chairs. But second, I wondered if the hand could still be re-attached. If it could move and spank and everything, maybe it could work normally if it was sewn back on Dad's wrist. I didn't know for sure. Hey, I'm not a doctor. But it certainly seemed worth a try.

So I started waiting for the hand at night. I'd lie there, pretending to sleep, making my breathing do that slow pattern that sounds like someone off in slumberland. It took a week, but finally, as I waited, I heard the click of nails on the wood in the hall followed by a creak as my door swung open. The scratching sound on the rug moved closer and closer to my bed.

I dove to the floor and made a grab, but the hand just managed to dodge from my clutches. I saw it dash through the doorway. I followed, running down the hall.

"What's all the noise about?" Dad asked, looking out from his bedroom.

"Your hand!" I shouted, pointing toward the steps.

Dad must have caught sight of it, because he joined in the chase. We ran down the steps. I nearly fell, but I managed to stay on my feet. The hand was just ahead of us. It went straight for the front hall. We had this cat door at the bottom of the regular door. The hand went right through it.

Dad and I followed the hand out to the yard.

"Got to catch it," I said.

"Yeah," Dad said.

The hand went around the side of the house and headed for the dock. We lived right next to a lake. We'd moved there because Dad liked to fish. He hadn't fished much in the last few weeks. We nearly caught up with the hand as it scampered toward the end of the dock.

"Stop," I shouted.

For an instant, the hand paused, as if listening to me. Then it dove into the water. Dad and I ran to the edge of the dock. We could see the hand swimming away.

"Come on," Dad said. He jumped into our little

boat. I joined him. The motor had a pull cord. I guess Dad couldn't handle it too well. He just pointed at it. I stepped past him and yanked the cord. The engine roared to life. I cranked it up to full speed and raced after the hand.

I guess it would have been better if I had waited for Dad to sit down. As I gunned the engine and turned the boat, Dad fell into the water. Then, when I tried to go back to help, the boat sort of went over him.

It's a good thing I'd taken that lifesaving course last year. By the time I got Dad onto the dock, Mom had called an ambulance. It could have been worse. He didn't get hit on the head or anything. But the blade from the propeller had cut him pretty badly. Actually, it had cut his foot right off. There was no chance of finding the foot in the water. But I had a pretty strong suspicion I'd be seeing it again. And feeling it.

# CRIZZLES

**N**ever let yourself get caught alone with a crizzle," Danny's grandpa told us that evening. It was the first thing he'd said to me since I'd arrived at Danny's place two hours earlier. Up until then, he'd just sat in his chair and stared out the window.

I looked at Danny, puzzled. He looked back at me and shrugged, then asked his grandpa, "What's a crizzle?"

"It's an awful thing," his grandpa said. "Looks just like a person. On the *outside*, that is. Looks just like you or me." He pointed at Danny, then at himself. "But inside, it's all dark and hungry. A crizzle lives for just one thing. A crizzle lives to get you alone and chomp your bones."

"How interesting," I said. "But we're a little old for fairy stories." I was hoping that he'd go back to ignoring us. I was in no mood to listen to him or any other adult. It was bad enough that I'd gotten into a fight with my folks. They're always bossing me around, and they're always trying to make me eat things I don't like. I can't believe the disgusting foods adults gobble up.

Well, I was sick of it, and I told them how I felt. Then Mom said if I didn't like it, I could find someone else to feed me. I was so angry I walked right out of the house with no idea where I was going. I'm not stupid, though—I grabbed a bag of cookies on the way through the kitchen. No way I was planning to go hungry.

I'd kept walking for a long time—long enough to eat all the cookies. I was almost at the edge of town when I realized how tired I was. But there was Danny's house, sitting at the end of the last side street before the woods. I barely knew him well enough to stop by, but he seemed happy to let me come in. Maybe he didn't have a lot of friends. The only problem was that Danny's parents were out, and that left us with Danny's grandpa. And once he'd gotten started, Grandpa didn't seem to want to stop talking.

"They get you alone," he said, "where no one can see. They don't even want another crizzle around when that special time comes. It's the way they are—very private. And then they change, like a candle dripping. The skin melts off and there's the crizzle, all mean and hungry. There's nothing nastier in the whole wide world. It's not a pretty thing. And if you see a crizzle, that's the last thing you'll see, let me tell ya, the last thing you'll see." He stretched forward in his chair and shouted, *"Chomp!"*

I jumped.

He started laughing.

"Very funny," I said, trying not to act embarrassed. I hadn't been scared, just startled. "Thanks for the fascinating story."

"Anyone want to go for a walk in the woods?" Grandpa asked.

"No thanks," I said.

He got up and shuffled to the window. "Beautiful night," he said. "Lovely night for a walk." He turned and stared at me. "Come on, young man. How about a little stroll?"

"No, thank you," I said. "It sounds absolutely wonderful, but I'm not sure I could handle the excitement." There was something hungry in the old man's eyes. I'd never admit that his silly story had spooked me, but there was no way I was going to go anywhere alone with him right now.

He took his hat and coat from a hook on the wall, then spoke to Danny. "Beautiful night, isn't it?"

"Yes, Grandpa," Danny said.

Danny's grandpa opened the door and gazed outside. "Ah, smell that night air. Nothing like a good long walk. Really helps build up an appetite."

Again, he stared at me. "Are you *sure* you don't want to go for a walk?"

"Maybe some other time."

"Suit yourself, but you don't know what you're missing." He stepped outside and closed the door. It shut with a clunk that shot through the room.

"Wow," I said, turning to Danny. "No offense, but your grandpa is kind of spooky. I could swear he was trying to get me alone."

Danny shook his head. "Nah, he wouldn't do that."

"How do you know?" I asked.

"He was just teasing," Danny told me. "He knew you wouldn't go with him."

I nodded. "You got that right."

"Besides, we take turns," Danny said. "Grandpa's real fair about that. And tonight, it's my turn." He grinned and winked at me.

"What?" I still didn't understand.

"Alone at last," Danny said. He started laughing. The grin spread wider as it dripped down his chin like stretched taffy.

I moved away until I felt the wall press against my back.

"Alone," he repeated. "Alone with a crizzle. Only one way that can turn out." Danny kept laughing as the flesh melted from his face like wax on a candle. And his eyes, even as they slid away to reveal what lay beneath, looked hungry. *Very* hungry.

# LIGHT AS A FEATHER, STIFF AS A BOARD

They'd been playing the game all summer, and it had sort of worked, but Sharon suspected they hadn't really done it right. Each evening kids from around the neighborhood would gather on one of the lawns, and they'd select a victim. Sharon believed it had to be someone heavy. With a light kid like Ray or Julie, it wasn't much of a trick. But with a heavier kid, they'd know if the game was real.

The group wasn't exactly the same each night, but there were certain kids who usually came. And there were certain kids who usually messed everything up. Billy, for instance, would do almost anything to get a laugh, even if it meant ruining the game.

Sharon had spent most of the day playing with Julie. Now she noticed that several kids had gathered half a block away on Kate's front yard. "Come on," she said to Julie.

"I don't know," Julie said. "I don't think I want to play."

"Why not?" Sharon took a step away from her friend. She had to join the others before the game started. Once they formed the circle, it would be too late.

Julie wrapped her arms around herself as if trying to hold onto her decision. "Kate's so bossy. I hate that."

"I know how you feel," Sharon said. She looked down the street anxiously. The game would start any minute. "Just don't pay any attention to her. It'll be fun. And it's the last day of vacation. You can't miss it."

Julie shook her head. "I really don't want to go."

"Please," Sharon said. "It won't be as much fun without you."

"Oh, all right," Julie said. "If it means that much to you." They walked down the street and gathered with the rest of the kids. Behind them the last of the sunlight melted away in puddles of red and purple against the sky. It would be dark soon.

Up ahead, Sharon saw that Kate had already taken charge of the group.

"Let's do it," Kate said.

Anne stretched out on the ground and crossed her arms over her chest. She closed her eyes.

"No," Kate said, poking Anne's arm. "You're too light. Get up."

Anne stood without arguing, but Sharon could tell that the girl was disappointed.

Kate scanned the group like a shopper looking for the nicest piece of meat in the display case. "Hmmm, what about Todd?"

"Sure," Todd said, grinning at the honor. He took Anne's place on the ground.

"I knew your weight would come in handy someday," Billy said.

Everyone gathered around Todd. Sharon knelt by his left leg. She could feel a change in the air as the kids grew serious.

Kate, kneeling by Todd's head, started the game.

"Light as a feather, stiff as a board," Kate said.

In a circle, starting at Kate's left, each of the others repeated the phrase: "Light as a feather, stiff as a board."

Sharon spoke when her turn came, making sure she sounded properly serious and somber. Each of the remaining kids took a turn, ending with Ray.

"Todd was in a car accident," Kate said as she sent the next phrase around the circle.

Again, they each repeated the words.

As Sharon took her turn, she heard Billy snicker.

When his turn came, Billy said, "Todd wet his pants."

It wasn't that funny, but Sharon giggled along with some of the other kids. Even Todd started laughing.

"That does it!" Kate shouted. She stood up and glared around the circle. Sharon looked away, feeling angry with herself for laughing and ruining the game.

"This is the last day of vacation," Kate said. "We get messed up every time. I want to do this right just once. You kids always ruin it. You," she said, pointing at Billy. "Out! You"—she pointed at Nora—"out! And you, too."

Sharon found herself staring at Kate's finger, hovering like a dagger just inches from her face. "But . . ."

"Out!" Kate screamed.

Sharon got up and backed away from the circle. It was a stupid game, anyway, she told herself. It never worked right. After chanting all the phrases, you were supposed to be able to lift the "victim" in the center with just two fingers. The victim was supposed to rise into the air. But there were so many kids playing that it was no big trick. It wasn't like the person really floated.

Julie started to get up to join Sharon. "Stay," Kate ordered. "We need you."

Julie stood, her eyes shifting back and forth between Sharon and Kate.

"We don't have enough," Kate said. "You'll ruin everything if you go. It will be all your fault."

"Go ahead," Sharon said to Julie.

"You sure?"

"Yeah."

Julie shrugged and rejoined the others on the ground.

"Light as a feather, stiff as a board," Kate began.

The chant went around the circle. Sharon watched, part of her hoping that someone would mess up but part of her wanting to see the game done perfectly just one time. She wasn't a member of the circle, but the chance to see it happen would still be special. She realized she'd lied to herself before—it wasn't just a stupid game. It was more than that. If it was done absolutely perfectly right, Sharon believed something wonderful would happen.

"Todd was in a car accident."

The chant made its path around the circle.

"Light as a feather, stiff as a board."

Perfect.

"Todd is in the hospital," Kate said.

Around it went.

"Light as a feather, stiff as a board."

As always in the game, the victim's condition grew worse with each turn.

"Todd is in a coma," Kate said.

It went around with no mistakes.

"Light as a feather, stiff as a board."

"Todd is dead," Kate said.

Each person in the circle repeated the phrase, quietly and seriously. The jokers were gone. Nobody seemed to want to ruin the magic this time. In the air that surrounded her, Sharon felt as if the night was listening, watching, waiting.

"Light as a feather, stiff as a board," Kate said.

The words took their path.

"Todd is in his coffin," Kate said.

The chant went around.

Kate started the last turn. "Light as a feather, stiff as a board." Her voice trembled slightly on the final word, but she spoke it clearly.

Sharon held her breath, wondering if the phrase would reach the end without error.

It did. For a moment, everyone in the circle remained still, as if they couldn't believe they'd succeeded. Then, all together, the group stood. Holding two fingers of each hand beneath Todd, they raised their hands. Light as a feather, Todd rose. They lifted their hands to shoulder height. Then they raised their hands above their heads, supporting Todd on their extended fingers. Finally, when they reached the limits that their bodies could stretch, they stopped.

But Todd didn't stop.

At first Sharon thought it was a trick of the moonlight. But Todd floated slowly above the outstretched arms.

"It worked," someone gasped.

"Stop him," Sharon shouted. She ran through

the circle of kids and leaped to catch hold of Todd. Her fingers brushed the back of his shirt, but he was too high for her to grab.

"Do something," Anne said.

Kate stood, staring up at Todd. "Stop that," she demanded. "Come down right now."

Todd continued to rise.

Sharon had an idea. "Do the whole thing backward," she said. "That might bring him down."

"I'll do it," Kate said as she pushed Sharon aside and knelt. "Quickly," she said. The others from the original circle joined her on the ground. Kate paused, moving her lips as if she was having a hard time working out the words. Finally, she said, "Board a as stiff, feather a as light."

"No, it all has to be backward," Sharon said.

Kate glared at her. "I just said it backward. Don't you know anything?"

"But it isn't all backward," Sharon said. "You still went first. You have to go last. And you have to go in the other direction and start with the last phrase."

"That makes sense," Julie said.

"Get out!" Kate yelled, pointing at Julie. "And you be quiet," she said, glaring at Sharon again.

Julie stood and joined Sharon. "It won't work," Sharon whispered to her. "I know it won't."

"Anyone else have anything to say?" Kate asked.

Nobody spoke.

"Board a as stiff, feather a as light," Kate said.

Sharon looked up. Todd was a dark splotch above her head. She hoped he would come down as slowly as he rose. But she was afraid it wouldn't work—not the way Kate was doing it.

"Accident car a in was Todd," Kate said, struggling to reverse each phrase.

But they were doing it without a mistake.

"Board a as stiff, feather a as light,"

Perfectly . . .

"Dead is Todd."

No mistakes . . .

"Board a as stiff, feather a as light."

Sharon fought the urge to shout, to stop them. "This is very wrong," she whispered to Julie.

Julie nodded. She seemed to know, too.

"Hospital the in is Todd."

"Board a as stiff, feather a as light."

"Coma a in is Todd."

"Board a as stiff, feather a as light."

"Coffin his in is Todd."

"Board a as stiff, feather a as light," Kate said for the very last time.

Each in the circle repeated the phrase.

They were done. Sharon raised her eyes to the night sky. Todd was now barely a smudged dot far over their heads, one dark star among all the bright ones. Sharon couldn't tell whether he was still rising.

"Is he coming down?" she asked Julie.

Julie didn't answer. Sharon felt a hand clutch her

shoulder, fingers digging painfully into her skin. "Hey, that hurts," she said as she jerked away.

Julie was pointing with her other hand and making sounds that weren't quite words.

Sharon looked to where Julie pointed. She, too, froze. The kids in the circle were still kneeling. But they were no longer on the ground. The whole group was rising. They rose silently, each one staring straight ahead as if locked in place.

Finally, Julie spoke. "They should have done it your way," she said.

"I guess so." Sharon watched as Kate and the others rose. She couldn't even see Todd anymore.

"Should we try to bring them down?" Julie asked.

Sharon shivered as the night grew cooler. She really didn't want all those kids to float away like chimney smoke. "If we do the game wrong, who knows what might happen to us?"

"Yeah," Julie said. "We could just float away, too."

Sharon nodded. "That's not all—think what will happen if we do it right."

"What?" Julie asked.

Sharon took one last look at the rising circle. "We'll get Kate back. And that would be even worse."

# THE EVIL TREE

ne day, as Patrick was walking home from school, he noticed a tree with a door in its side. He'd walked past this same tree many times, but there had never been a door before. A man stood next to the tree. He looked like a soldier, but he wasn't wearing a uniform. He wore black pants and a black shirt with black buttons. The only color in his outfit was a gold buckle on his belt in the shape of a shield. His black hair was cut short. The man stood straight and stiff, but his eyes scanned slowly back and forth as if he was waiting for someone.

"What's this?" Patrick asked, pointing to the door. It looked like a small version of a castle door. It was built with planks of wood. That was the only part that made sense to Patrick—if a tree had a door, the door should be made of wood. The planks were braced with crossbars of iron. There were large hinges on the left side and a heavy bolt on the right.

The man didn't say anything.

"What is this?" Patrick asked again.

"You don't want to know," the man said.

"Yes, I do," Patrick said. He took a step backward, remembering that he wasn't supposed to talk to strangers.

"I really shouldn't tell you." The man turned his head away, as if pretending that Patrick didn't exist.

"Tell me," Patrick demanded. "Or . . ." He paused, trying to find the perfect threat. Sometimes he had to shout, sometimes he had to beg, and sometimes he had to whine. Sometimes he even had to pretend to be nice. But he always found a way to get whatever he desired. A ripple of excitement raced through Patrick as he thought of the perfect words. "Tell me or I'll scream that you tried to kidnap me."

"Would you really do something so nasty?" the man asked, still facing away from Patrick.

"Do you want to find out?" Patrick almost hoped he'd have a chance to start shouting.

The man sighed and turned back toward Patrick. "Very well. I'll tell you. But you must promise not to reveal my secret to anyone. Do you swear?"

"I swear," Patrick said. That was no problem. He'd grown very good at making promises, even when he had no intention of keeping them.

The man leaned forward and whispered. Patrick strained to hear. "Evil," the man said. "This is where evil is stored to keep it away from the innocent people of the world."

"You're crazy." Patrick enjoyed the chance to be rude to this stranger.

"Perhaps," the man said. "But I am one of the guardians who have been given the task of protecting the world from evil."

"Yeah, right." Patrick was nearly certain that the man was crazy. But he couldn't walk away without finding out for sure. If the man was telling the truth, there could be something fabulous inside the tree. Patrick wondered what evil looked like—did it have claws or wings? Did it have snakes for hair? He wasn't afraid of such things—he was attracted to them. He had to see what was behind the door.

There was no reason to ask. It would be easier to just *take* what he wanted.

Patrick dashed forward and grabbed the bolt. He slid it free, then yanked hard. The door opened so fast Patrick almost lost his balance. He held onto the bolt and steadied himself, eager to see the evil.

There was nothing inside the tree.

"Hey, it's empty," Patrick said. He felt his jaws tighten as he gritted his teeth. It was all just some kind of stupid joke. The man would pay for tricking him. "You liar!" he screamed. "You stinking liar! This doesn't hold any evil!" Patrick's mind raced to find the best way to get even with the man.

With surprising suddenness and strength, the man pushed Patrick. He lost his grip on the edge of the door and stumbled inside the tree. "This doesn't hold any evil!" Patrick shouted again as the door slammed shut, sealing the chamber in darkness. From outside, he heard three words.

"Now it does."

There was a scraping sound as the bolt slid into place. Then Patrick heard quiet footsteps, fading, fading away.

# KIDZILLA

hen I woke up this morning, I was a lizard. I realized something was wrong the moment I rolled out of bed. The frame of the bed broke under my weight. I jumped as the mattress crashed to the floor, but I jumped too high, cracking my head on the ceiling and cracking the ceiling with my head. At the same time, my tail lashed the wall, knocking a large hole next to the window and spreading a shower of plaster. That made me sneeze, and I blew another hole in the wall.

"Hey, what's going on up there?" Dad shouted from below.

"Nothing," I tried to say. But it came out

*"Arrrrannnggg."* This situation definitely had possibilities.

"Just keep it down," Dad said.

I made my way into the hall, doing only a little damage to one side of the door frame. I wish I could say the same about the toilet, but it shattered under the force of my you-know-what. Personal hygiene proved to be a challenge. I discovered I could pick up my toothbrush if I clutched it between both claws. It took almost the whole tube to clean all my teeth, but at least when I was done my mouth felt minty fresh. You wouldn't believe how bad a lizard's mouth can taste first thing in the morning.

Breakfast time.

I was hungry enough to eat a house.

Mom was making pancakes. "Hi, hon," she said as I crashed my way into the kitchen and crushed down onto a chair. "Help yourself to juice." She slid a plate stacked with pancakes onto the table.

I looked at the fridge and at my claws. The juice just didn't seem worth the effort. Luckily, I was able to hook the pancakes without too much trouble. They tasted so good, I even licked my claws.

"Oops," Mom said, glancing up at the clock. "Better get moving. You don't want to be late for school."

"Yes, Mom," I said. It came out as a low growl, along with a stream of fire that shot across the kitchen and melted the garbage can. Oops.

I snagged my backpack with one claw and went through the door. The warm sunlight felt great on my scales. As soon as I crashed through the front gate, I learned that the sidewalk along the street was made of pretty thin concrete. The stuff just crumbled under my feet. It was like walking on Rice Krispies. Actually, it made a pretty neat sound.

I was having so much fun crunching the concrete that I was almost late for school. The bell was just ringing when I smashed through the narrow door.

Sitting at one of those tiny desks was out of the question, so I stood in the back of the room. When Mrs. Franzski came in, she just glanced over at me and said, "Oh, Bradley, I see you've found a new spot. Well, as long as you're comfortable."

She was very big on making sure we all had the proper "learning environment." She even let Danny Mitty sit on the floor sometimes.

I didn't raise my claw during class. I was pretty sure that if I said anything, I might be unable to avoid adding a stream of fire that would fry some of my classmates. While I wasn't exactly buddy-buddy with everyone, there weren't any kids who'd done anything bad enough to deserve being flamed.

After our reading lesson, we had gym class. We were doing our physical fitness tests today, so my size and strength came in pretty handy. I ran faster than ever before. Even though I had tiny arms, my powerful shoulders allowed me to do great at pushups. I did well at everything except sit-ups. Somehow, I just wasn't built for them.

The rest of the morning went fairly smoothly. Lunch, however, looked like it might be a problem. They always served these really small portions in the cafeteria. Here I was, starving, ravenous, monstrously hungry, and the lady behind the counter plops this tiny little scoop of chicken surprise on my plate. Sorry. Not enough. I reached over the counter and grabbed the whole pan. Let me tell you—I must have been starving. Even the chicken surprise looked good. And, compared to the normal taste inside a lizard's mouth, it wasn't all that bad, either.

Back in class, I wondered whether there was any point in paying attention. I mean, my future was pretty much not going to be changed by my ability or inability to name all the state capitals. The career options for giant lizards would be more along the lines of knocking down buildings or making tunnels through mountains. But I'd been a kid all my life and a lizard for just a day. Old habits are hard to break and old fears are very powerful. So I stayed in class.

As we were leaving the room at the end of the day, Mrs. Franzski called to me. "Bradley, you didn't seem to be with us today. I hope you can pay more attention tomorrow."

"Sure," I said, though it came out as a bit of a roar.

She smiled, then went back to grading papers.

I headed home, walking along the same trail of crumbled sidewalk. Mom was making dinner. Dad was still at work. I went up to my room and melted all my toy soldiers, one at a time, with little puffs of breath. I hadn't played with them in years, so it was no big deal if I ruined them.

Dinner went pretty much like breakfast. It was fried chicken, so Mom didn't make a fuss when I ate with my hands. Lucky thing she hadn't made meat loaf—or soup.

I slept really well. All that crushing and crashing must have tired me out. When I woke, I got out of bed carefully. But I realized I didn't have to be very cautious. I wasn't a lizard anymore. This morning, I was a robot. Good thing, too. We're having a math test today.

# EVERYONE'S A WINNER

"COME-UH, COME-UH, COME-UH! COME AND TRY YER LUCK." The shout of the barker rang over the thousand other noises filling the cotton-candy air of the traveling carnival. "You there; yeah, you," he called as he leaned forward and pointed at Derek. "Give it a try."

Derek paused. He knew he should have kept walking, but he couldn't ignore someone who was talking to him. It was a curse. He was too polite. "No thanks," he said, a half smile nervously spreading across his lips.

"Everyone's a winner," the barker said. "Come on, what are you afraid of? I won't bite you."

Derek shrugged. What was he afraid of? It was

only a game. Just skee ball, as a matter of fact. It looked easy enough to beat the score—250 points for a small prize, 300 for a medium, and a tough 420 for a large. Heck, Derek was sure he could hit 250 standing backward and tossing with his left hand. He dug in his pocket past the crumpled ride tickets and gum wrappers until his fingers found a quarter.

"That's the way," the barker said. "You can't win if you don't play."

Derek dropped the quarter in the slot. It hung for a second before being swallowed by the machine. There was a clunk, followed by the rumble of the nine balls rolling down toward Derek. He began to play. Derek winced as he got off to a bad start. The first shot was pretty poor. He took a breath and looked around. Nobody was paying the slightest attention to him. He rolled another lousy shot into the ten-point hole. Then he hit a thirty.

"Guess I needed to warm up," he said, half to himself and half to the barker. His next couple of rolls weren't bad. He hit a thirty and two forties, then rolled three balls in a row perfectly for fifties.

*Twenty more,* Derek thought, holding the last ball in his hand. He was at 280, more than enough for a small prize, but he knew it would be junk. An easy twenty points and he'd move up from totally worthless junk to worthless junk, or maybe even just plain old junk. *Nice and easy,* Derek thought as he swung the ball.

"COME-UH, COME-UH!"

Startled by the shout, Derek jerked his hand forward. The ball shot from his grip, bounced toward the targets, and plopped into the ten-point hole.

"A WINNER!" The man handed him a piece of green plastic. "Two-ninety. Small prize. Congratulations, kid. You're a real champ."

Derek turned the piece of plastic over in his hand and stared at it. "What's this?"

"A bracelet. You can trade up for more prizes. Play again?"

Derek was about to answer when he was shoved aside. "I'll try." A kid—a big, ugly, mean-looking kid—barged in front of Derek and jammed a quarter in the slot with a grubby hand.

"Everyone's a winner," the barker said, smiling. "And you're just in time for our scoring special." He reached up and flipped over the sign that displayed the prize scores.

"But—" Derek stepped back. He couldn't believe it—only 150 points for a small prize, and 200 for a medium. *Forget it,* he told himself. *There's always a trick. They never let you win anything good.* He stepped back another pace but kept watching. The kid stunk. He rolled mostly twenties, with a couple of lucky thirties. He ended up with 200 points.

"We have a winner!" The barker handed the kid a small stuffed animal.

Derek shook his head. Some people had all the

luck. There was no way he was going to wait around for another turn if he had to watch this kid win prizes. He decided to ride the Spin-a-Thon again. That was more his speed. It was scary—not because the ride was so rough, but because all the equipment in the carnival looked like it was within half an inch of breaking down. Every time he took a seat on that rusty old ride, Derek couldn't help imagining the door flying open—or maybe the whole car just breaking off the shaft and hurtling through the air, carrying Derek like some medieval catapult boulder, rolling and tumbling as the crowd below screamed in panic. Yeah, the Spin-a-Thon sounded good.

The ride, as always, was uneventful. When Derek got off, he found himself walking past the skee ball booth again. The kid was still there. He was playing furiously, throwing ball after ball without pausing between shots. His shirt was soaked from the effort. Sweat dripped from his hair at the back of his neck. Sweat flew when he shook his head after each throw. A pile of stuffed animals lay at his feet.

Derek stopped to watch. "WINNER!" the barker shouted. "Medium prize," he said. He handed the kid another stuffed animal. "Medium also wins a free play." He reached down and pressed a button.

Derek heard the balls rolling out. *Darn,* he thought. *That could have been me.* If the kid got a free play each time he hit 200, he'd be playing forever. Derek would have loved another chance—

especially with those easy scores. He knew he could hit 200 points. But the kid wasn't going to move. He was just going to stand there and win all the prizes.

Derek looked around for something else to do. There was a wagon set back a bit past the skee ball. A large sign in faded letters proclaimed BOBO, THE MAN-EATING MONSTER!!!

Derek knew it would be a rip-off. It would be a guy in a gorilla suit, or a mechanical dummy covered with fur, or some other kind of trick. But he was getting bored, and admission probably only cost half a buck. Derek was willing to waste a couple of quarters. He walked up the ramp to the front of the wagon. There was nobody at the ticket window.

"Hello?" Derek tried to look past the bars. "Hello? Anybody here?" He waited a moment, then moved to the door that was next to the window. He was about to call again when he heard people arguing inside the wagon.

"He has to be fed," the first voice said. It was a woman speaking.

"We fed him last week," a man said. "It's too soon. We can't have a pattern."

"Look, Charlie is already setting it up. Didn't you see him flip the sign? Besides, nobody ever remembers. Bobo will see to that."

"I wish I knew how Bobo did that," the man said. "I still can't believe the way the crowd forgets everything."

"It's not important how he does it," the woman said. "What matters is if he doesn't get fed, he might decide to change our deal. I wouldn't want him thinking about us as dinner."

"Okay," the man said, "I guess you're right. Let him loose."

"Bobo," the woman called. "Dinner time." There was a rattling of chains, then a screech of animal joy.

Derek had heard enough. He started to back away from the door and down the ramp. He stumbled, tripping over the edge of a plank. Derek twisted his body as he fell, landing hard on his side.

"What was that?" he heard the woman ask.

"Doesn't matter right now," the man said. "Go get it, Bobo."

Derek felt the ramp shake, *thump-clunk, thump-clunk*. Something big was coming out. Something large and mean and hungry. He jumped up. A sharp pain shot through his ankle, nearly dropping him again. Behind him, a huge creature was squeezing through the door. Derek saw brown, leathery hide with patches of black fur. A smell like dead meat wafted over him. He almost threw up.

People in the crowd were looking at the trailer. Some of them ran. Others just kept staring. Then Bobo burst out and everyone was running and screaming.

Derek tried to run, but the pain searing through his ankle was so bad he almost passed out. Behind him, Bobo stood erect. He was as tall as the wagon. Bobo, like some nightmare cross between an ape and a lizard, was coming after him.

Derek hobbled away from the trailer. Ahead, he saw the skee ball game. In the middle of all the panic, two people weren't running. The kid was bending down to scoop up his stuffed animals. The barker was leaning against the side of the booth as if nothing special was happening.

The pain in Derek's ankle felt worse than anything he could ever have imagined—worse than the time he hit the curb with his bike and flew off, sliding across the sidewalk on both knees. Worse than the time he'd slammed his finger in the car door. But the thought of being Bobo's dinner was far worse than the pain that shot through his ankle. He pushed himself as much as he could without passing out.

Derek glanced back at the wagon. Bobo had clumped down to the bottom of the ramp. The creature shot a hungry look to either side, then stared straight at Derek. Bobo lurched toward him. Derek gritted his teeth and forced himself to go faster.

The kid, the one with all the stuffed animals, was right in Derek's path. Derek tried to go around. The kid was still fumbling with the animals. He dropped one. Derek hobbled past him, fire running up his leg and exploding in his brain.

He took several agonizing steps, then looked back. The kid straightened up, but a couple of the stuffed animals fell from his arms. He bent down and grabbed one of his prizes. A few more tumbled out of his grip. He'd won more prizes than he could possibly hold.

"Run!" Derek shouted at him.

The kid raised his head briefly, his face blank and empty, then looked back at the ground and tried to gather more of his winnings. Bobo was right behind him. The carnival beast raised a claw and swiped. Stuffed animals flew in a shower.

Everything slowed down for Derek, as if he was watching someone else's dream. A soft object struck his chest. He clutched at it. A woman was behind Bobo. She said several words to the barker. It might have been, "Good job, Charlie."

"This one will hold him for a while," Charlie might have said. "Atta boy, Bobo. Take him inside. Good Bobo."

Around Derek, the crowd stopped running and screaming. The people stood for a moment, then shrugged or shook their heads and went back to their rides and games and food. After a while, Derek couldn't even remember what everyone had been so excited about.

"How was the carnival?" Derek's mom asked when he got home.

"Not bad." He limped into the living room.

"Did you hurt yourself?"

*Hurt myself?* Derek realized he must have twisted his ankle coming up the stairs. "I'm okay."

"Did you win that?" his mom asked.

Derek looked at the stuffed animal he was gripping. "Yeah, I guess so."

"They sure are giving away ugly prizes," his mom said.

Derek examined the animal. It was such a piece of junk, he couldn't even tell what it was supposed to be. Maybe it was a gorilla. It might even have been a lizard. It certainly didn't look like anything he'd ever seen before. *Well,* he thought as he carried his prize up to his room, *at least I won something.*

# A LITTLE OFF THE TOP

**R**yan checked his pocket to make sure he hadn't lost the money his mother had given him. It was still there. He hesitated at the door of the barbershop, wondering whether he could come up with any good excuse for skipping the whole unpleasant experience. Nothing came to mind. Best just to get it over with, he thought as he stepped inside. Life would be a lot easier if hair didn't grow so quickly. Ryan didn't like any part of going to the barbershop. He didn't like waiting for his turn, and he didn't like sitting in the chair, and he didn't like having his head moved and turned and twisted as Mr. Garafolo snipped at his hair.

"I'm here for my usual," Ryan said.

Mr. Garafolo turned toward Ryan. But it wasn't Mr. Garafolo—it was a different man. He was dressed the same, with the white shirt and black pants, and he held a pair of scissors in his hand, but he was not Mr. Garafolo. The barber rotated the empty chair toward Ryan. "Step right up."

"Uh, where's Mr. Garafolo?" Ryan asked.

"Tony's unavailable," the man said. "I'm his cousin, Vince Sweeny. Come on, you'll like the way I cut hair. You'll leave here with a big smile. You'll be grinning from ear to ear. I promise."

Ryan noticed there were no other customers in the shop. He wondered if this barber had scared them off by giving someone a bad haircut. "Maybe I should come back later . . ."

"No, no. Come on. Tony would want it this way," Mr. Sweeny said, pointing to the chair with his scissors. "Please."

"Okay," Ryan said. He noticed the way the hair clippings scattered in the breeze his feet made as they clomped on the old linoleum. It almost seemed as if the clippings were running from him.

Ryan climbed into the chair. The barber draped a large cloth over him and tied it around his neck. Ryan didn't know why barbers bothered with that sheet—the hairs always managed to sneak through and make him itch for hours after getting a cut.

"Now," the barber said, "how would you like it? Short? Medium? Are you one of those kids with the short top and long sides? You tell me."

"Short is good," Ryan said. He looked down at the cloth. There was a stain. It was dark red, almost brown. He stared at the splotch, wondering if it was blood.

Suddenly, hands grabbed his head and bent it back.

"Ah, that's better," the barber said. "Keep your head nice and straight. You don't want to wiggle around."

"Sorry," Ryan said.

The barber started snipping away at Ryan's head. Bits of hair went flying. Bits of hair, somehow, got through the collar. The barber pushed Ryan's head forward. Ryan raised his eyes and looked into the mirror. There was a door at the back of the shop, leading to a storage room. In the reflection of the rear wall, a foot stuck out on the floor by the door. *A foot?* Ryan started to turn his head.

"Sit still," the barber said, clamping his hands on Ryan's head and twisting it away from the mirror. "Keep still. I wouldn't want to cut you." The hand held hard and firm for a moment, then let go. "That's a good boy."

Ryan swallowed, trying not to move his head at all. *Who was this man?* Ryan realized he didn't know anything about the person who was standing behind him with the sharp, pointed scissors. He didn't even know for sure if the man was Mr. Garafolo's cousin, or if he was a real barber.

He glanced at the cash register. The drawer was half open.

*Maybe the man wasn't a barber at all.*

Shifting his eyes far to the right, Ryan could just see the image in the mirror. For sure, it was a foot—there was a black shoe and the edge of a black pants cuff, like the black pants the barber wore. Like the black pants Mr. Garafolo wore.

The scissors moved close to his ear, making tiny snips. "Where did you say Mr. Garafolo was?" Ryan asked.

*Snip!*

Ryan jumped as the scissors took off a large hunk of hair right next to his ear.

"Easy, don't jump. You want to lose your ear?" The barber put his hand on Ryan's head again. He kept snipping, but he didn't answer Ryan's question.

Ryan clenched his fists under the sheet and closed his eyes.

"Relax," the barber said. "You'll be finished soon."

Ryan took a deep breath. It didn't help. There was no way he could relax, not with a body in the back room and this cold-blooded killer standing behind him.

"Just another snip, then a little touch-up with the razor," the barber said.

*Razor?* Ryan grabbed the arms of the chair and opened his eyes.

He flinched as the barber slapped shaving cream on the back of his neck. It felt warm and wet. Ryan could almost imagine that it was blood. He looked down at the splotch on the sheet again. There was a scritch-scratch sound as the barber sharpened the razor on the strop hanging from the chair.

From the corner of his eye, Ryan caught sight of motion in the mirror. The foot was twitching—he was sure of it. Then, from the room, he heard a scream, "Eeeeooowwwwerrr!"

Ryan ripped the sheet from his neck, jumped from the chair, and spun to face the barber.

"Hey, careful!" The barber threw his hand up, the razor gleaming as bits of lather flew into the air. "This thing is sharp. It could take your head right off."

Ryan tried to run but his feet tangled in the sheet. He hit the ground. There was another awful scream from the next room, "Eeeeoooowwwaaggghhh."

Lying on his side, tangled in the sheet, Ryan saw the foot move. It pulled back into the room. Ryan looked up. Mr. Garafolo stumbled out from the back room. Ryan expected to see him grab his throat and fall to the floor. But the barber was just stretching and yawning, making a sound like "Eeeeoooowwarrgleee."

Mr. Garafolo glanced at the empty chair. Then he stared at the floor. "Ryan. What's the matter? You don't like the way Vince cuts hair?"

"Uh . . ." Ryan untangled himself from the sheet, stood up, and plopped into the chair. "He does a great job."

"You're a nice boy, Ryan," Mr. Garafolo said, "but you are a little jumpy. Try to relax. You'll live longer." He turned to Vince and said, "Thanks for letting me take a nap. The doctor was right—my back feels a lot better when I sleep on a hard floor. You can go now. I'll finish Ryan."

*Finish me?* Ryan thought. He started to leap from the chair again.

"Calm down," Mr. Garafolo said, clamping a hand on Ryan's shoulder. "This is supposed to be a pleasure."

Ryan tried not to flinch as the razor scraped across the back of his neck.

"Okay," Mr. Garafolo said a minute later. "All done."

Ryan paid Mr. Garafolo and walked out of the shop. "Come back soon," he heard Mr. Garafolo call as the door closed behind him.

Ryan took a deep breath. It felt great to be standing in the bright sun and fresh air.

What a perfect day, Ryan thought as he walked down the street. It would be a perfect and wonderful and stunningly great day, except for one small thing. Now that he was done with the barber, it was time for his appointment at the dentist. Running his hand through his hair and gritting his teeth, Ryan headed across town.

# THE SLIDE

**K**ay plopped down on the bench at the edge of the playground and set Tommy loose. "Go play," she said as she took a can of soda out of her backpack. "Have fun. Don't get hurt." She watched him scurry off to the monkey bars. All around, she saw little kids having mindless fun, running and laughing and squealing like upright pigs.

"Unbelievable," Kay said to herself.

She had dragged Tommy all around town, then just picked a direction and started walking, hoping he would be exhausted enough to sleep most of the afternoon once she got him back to his house. If he slept, she'd be free to hang out and watch TV.

But she couldn't take him home for another hour.

His mother had explained that she needed her *personal time* each morning. Kay had to keep Tommy out of the house until noon. It was part of her job.

Kay hated playgrounds, but she got paid the same cheap baby-sitting rate whether she read to the little creature or played with him or just set him loose to romp and frolic. She saw no point working herself ragged for a couple of dollars an hour.

Kay tried to remember if she'd visited this playground before. She'd been watching Tommy almost every day for these first three weeks of summer, and she'd dragged the sticky little nose-picker to a lot of places. They'd all looked pretty much the same. This one was a bit shabbier than some. But it wasn't like any of the equipment was actually dangerous. It wouldn't do to bring the little bug home with broken parts. Kay suspected Mrs. Walton wouldn't pay her if her precious Tommy snapped an arm or a leg or cut his forehead open on a rusty piece of jagged metal.

There didn't seem to be any danger of that at the moment. The monkey bars looked safe enough to Kay. The little cockroach wasn't so high up that a fall would fracture anything important. Kay settled back on the bench and glanced around. Usually there were other sitters to talk to. Not today.

Next to the bench, Kay saw a garbage barrel, and next to that another large barrel for aluminum cans. A sign on the second barrel read: PLEASE RECYCLE. Kay sipped the last drops of her soda, then tossed the can toward the barrels. It hit the rim of one, then bounced to the ground. Kay laughed. It didn't matter if she missed—someone would pick it up. That was the nice thing about recycling, as far as Kay was concerned—there was always someone willing to step in and do the job.

No matter how unpleasant a job, there was always someone who would do it . . . for a price. Kay knew she was living proof of that theory. But there were lots of worse things in life than watching a slimy little grub run around. And it wasn't like she'd be doing it the rest of her life.

Kay looked at the piece of equipment nearest her bench. It was one of those tube slides—a big, slanted plastic tube with a ladder at one end. The middle of the tube was held up from the ground on another short tube. A little kid was just springing out the bottom. Kay watched him slide to the ground and land on his feet. His untied sneakers hit the dirt with a *plock*. He bent his knees, taking the jolt like an expert, and ran off. A moment later, a second kid came out. *Plock*. Kay glanced at the top—there were no other kids waiting to enter the slide.

For a moment, Kay thought about going through the slide herself. It almost looked like fun. But she was too old for that. And what if one of her friends saw her? She'd never live it down.

"Kay! Watch me!" Tommy screamed from the monkey bars. He was hanging from a bar at one corner, swinging his body and kicking his legs. Kay turned her head his way for a moment. She didn't even bother trying to appear interested. The little worm seemed satisfied just to have her eyes aimed in his direction.

*Plock.* Another kid had just come out of the tube slide. Like the first two, he hit the ground with both feet and went running off.

Kay hadn't noticed him at the top of the ladder. She realized the kid must have climbed in when she'd looked toward Tommy. For all the noise they usually made, there were times when little kids could move as silently as spiders.

"Push me, Kay!" Tommy called as he ran from the monkey bars to the swings. "Push me! Push me! Push me! Push me!"

"They don't pay me enough for this," Kay muttered as she trudged over to him. She noticed that there were a lot of kids in the playground. They all looked the same, except for Tommy, who was a stupid little four-year-old dressed in jeans and a red shirt. The rest of them were mostly stupid little four-year-olds dressed in jeans and blue shirts.

Kay gave Tommy a push, resisting the urge to shove the ridiculous creature right off the swing, then went back to the bench. As she sat, another kid came out of the slide. He hit—*plock*—stood for a second as if figuring out where he was, then went running off to the seesaws.

Kay could have sworn she hadn't seen anyone go in the top. She got up and walked to the slide, then bent to look inside the bottom of the tube. An odd smell drifted out, moist and old, like the scent of earth beneath a rock. Kay could barely make out a dark place where the slide rested on the support tube. It almost looked like a hole, but she knew that couldn't be right. If there were a hole in the middle, the kids would fall in.

Unless . . .

Kay had a glimmer of an idea, but it was too strange. She let it go and went back to the bench. Tommy came running over. "Play seesaw with me," he demanded.

Kay shook her head. The last thing she wanted was a seat full of splinters. "Why don't you make some friends?" she suggested.

"They don't like me," Tommy said.

Now there's a surprise, Kay thought. But all she said was, "Go back to the swings. Practice pumping. I'll be right here."

Tommy ran off. Kay watched as he wove his way around the other kids, keeping as much distance from each of them as possible. It reminded her of a video game.

A moment later, another kid came sliding out of the end of the tube. *Plock*. The place was crawling with kids. Kay was sure it was more crowded now. There were kids piled on the seesaws and the swings and all over the climbing equipment. There were kids running around chasing each other in a nonstop game of tag. But there weren't any parents or sitters in sight. Kay glanced at the parking lot next to the playground. It was empty. She thought about leaving. Tommy would pitch a fit. But he'd do that whether they left now, or in ten minutes, or in ten hours.

Kay checked her watch. It was only a few minutes after eleven. She figured she'd wait another half hour, then drag Tommy home. With luck, he'd be tired by then.

As Kay sat and waited for time to pass, she noticed something odd. There weren't any girls in the playground. Kay looked around to make sure she wasn't mistaken. As she did, another little kid popped out from the end of the tube slide. It was a boy. He looked just like all the others.

It was almost as if— No, she dropped that thought. It was too ridiculous.

"Don't be silly," she whispered. Kay shifted uncomfortably on the bench. Maybe it was time to leave.

Another kid came out of the slide.

Maybe it was time to leave *right now*.

Yes. Time to get Tommy and head home, Kay thought. It was definitely time to get out.

*Plock*. Two more feet hit the dirt in front of the slide.

Kay jumped up from the bench. The playground was swarming with kids. They were everywhere. Everywhere except the top of the slide, Kay realized. She was certain she hadn't seen a single one of those kids go in the top.

They all just slid out the bottom.

It was almost like . . . She took a deep breath, not wanting to think about that image but unable to keep her mind from turning down that dark corner—*almost like insects*. Kay shivered as she remembered a film she'd seen in science class. In a disgustingly large close-up shot, a swollen termite queen was popping out one egg after another. Smooth, slimy, white eggs squeezed out. *Plock.* Thousands of them. *Plock, plock, plock.* Kay couldn't wipe the image from her mind. She knew what was happening. Instead of eggs, the tube was plocking out snotty little kids, creating thousands of workers to serve its needs.

"That's crazy," Kay said.

She started to move away from the bench.

"Kay, look at me!" Tommy shouted from high up on the swings.

Kay hesitated. She wanted to run from the playground, but there'd be big trouble if she left Tommy. She stepped toward him.

Kids swarmed forward and blocked her way. Another kid slid from the slide. *Plock*—his feet hit the dirt. The mob moved closer. They were all around her. Except for the swing that held Tommy, the equipment was empty. They'd all left the swings and seesaws and monkey bars to gather around her. Kay could feel them pushing in from the sides and from behind.

Insects, Kay thought as she stared into the empty faces of little kids closing in around her. They pressed closer. They all looked the same, and none of them looked quite right. This close, Kay saw that their arms were a bit too long, their heads a bit too small. The skin of their fingers as they grasped at her was slippery and wet.

*Plock.* Another kid came from the slide. *Plock. Plock.* Two more.

Kay was sure, now.

They surged against her. They shoved. They herded. They lifted her. Kay grabbed the bench, struggling to keep her feet on the ground. They pried her fingers loose and raised her over their heads. Dozens of hands held her up in the air.

"No!" Kay screamed.

They carried her toward the slide.

"Not there!" Kay tried to twist from their grip. "Please, not there . . ."

None of the kids spoke. But all together, they produced a droning buzz that filled her ears.

Across the playground, Tommy was still swinging, trying to pump himself higher.

*Little rat,* Kay thought. *No,* she realized. He wasn't a rat. He was an insect. They were all insects.

They hauled her toward the top of the slide. Behind her, more were born. *Plock. Plock. Plock.* They lifted her higher, crawling on top of each other to form a mound. The droning buzz grew louder and louder until it filled her head and made her body vibrate. The tube swallowed the sunlight as Kay slid in. She clutched at the edge for an instant, but a dozen tiny hands pushed her deeper.

Kay lost her grip. She slid. Halfway down, she fell into a hole. For an instant, Kay remembered the high dive, and the stomach-lurching feeling of plummeting toward the water.

Kay dropped.

Her fall ended far too soon. She hit something large and soft and moist, like a giant, living wound. Kay sank. Ankles, knees, then thighs slipped into the goo. It was a huge insect, Kay realized, living in darkness, too swollen to move, buried in a hive beneath the playground, producing countless insect children. Here it waited, fat and slow and blind.

Beneath her, in a voice that came right into her mind, she heard a huge and old and terribly strange life-form speak.

"Oh, good," it said. "You are here. Good. Thank you, my children."

Kay sank deeper into the moist mass of flesh. All around, she could feel the little ones emerging, scrambling out and climbing toward the tube that led to the middle of the slide.

Kay's last thought almost made her laugh. This creature was about to absorb her, using her to create more of its own kind. She realized she was about to be recycled.

Somewhere outside and above, the buzz of the children drowned out any sounds Kay made.

# BIG KIDS

**M**y friend Stu is scared of just about everything. He's almost a year younger than me. I guess that makes a difference, because he's always saying "Watch out for this," or "Look out for that." He's especially scared of the Big Kids. He'll say, "Don't go in there, Danny, the Big Kids will get you," or, "We'd better leave before some Big Kids come."

I don't see what the problem is—I'll bet I could outrun any Big Kid. I could probably outfight most of them, too. Not that I want to find out . . .

We'd been swimming in the quarry that day. Actually, *I'd* been swimming. Stu was too chicken to go into the water. He was afraid he'd get a cramp and drown, or that some girls would come along and see him in his underwear. So I was swimming and Stu was sitting. That's when I got the idea. "Hey, Stu," I said, treading water.

"Yeah?" He glanced up from the stick he was peeling.

"It's too hot here. Let's go to the caves."

He stared at me like I had suggested we jump off a bridge. "No way. There might be Big Kids there."

"Come on, nobody goes there. It'll be great."

Stu shook his head. I got out of the water and climbed up the steep bank. In a few minutes, the hot sun had dried me better than any towel could. "Come on, the caves."

"No."

"Come on. Are you chicken? Let's go."

Stu shook his head. "I don't want to."

I put on my jeans and shirt. "I'm going. You do what you want." I'd learned that trick from my parents. I started walking. In a few seconds, I heard Stu running to catch up.

"But what if there are—"

"No problem. I'll deal with anything that comes up." After all this talk, I was almost hoping to run into some Big Kids. I'd show Stu there was nothing to worry about.

Stu jabbered a bit more on the way to the caves, but I didn't pay much attention. He hung back when I reached the entrance. I went ahead without waiting for him. It got dark pretty quickly, but there were enough cracks and openings that the passageways never got completely black. I figured Stu would catch up with me in a minute. I went a few feet farther, then stopped, expecting to hear Stu chugging up behind me. Instead, I heard a shout.

"Ow!"

I ran back to the entrance. Wouldn't you know that bad stuff always happens to whoever expects it to happen? I think if you're afraid enough of something and worry enough, it almost has to happen. So there was Stu, caught by the one thing he feared the most. Yup, the Big Kids had him. They formed a ring around Stu and were pushing him back and forth, like a game of human hot potato. His face was pretty much frozen with terror and red enough to use for a stop sign.

I figured I could wait and see how bad it got, or I could rush in now and try to help him. So far, they were just pushing. There was a good chance they'd get bored with Stu and leave him in a minute or two.

I'd forgotten that Big Kids can get really cruel when they're bored.

One of them hit Stu a hard shot to the stomach. "Ooff," Stu grunted. He doubled over and staggered back, crashing into the Big Kid who was closest to the mouth of the cave.

I was moving before I even realized what was happening.

As the Big Kid stumbled from the impact, I

stuck my foot out behind him. He went over backward. I reached out, grabbed Stu by the arm, and yanked.

"Huh?" he cried out.

"Shut up and run." I pushed Stu ahead of me. The surprise was worth a few seconds' head start. There was a good chance we could escape.

"Get them!" one of the Big Kids shouted from behind us.

Stu was whimpering, but he kept up his speed. I herded him, taking the familiar turns. I really knew the caves as well as anyone.

At least, I thought I did.

After a while, the sound of the Big Kids' footsteps faded. We'd escaped. At worst, they'd be waiting at the mouth of the cave. But they wouldn't stay there forever. They'd get tired of waiting, and they'd leave.

"Thanks," Stu said quietly when we stopped running.

"Anytime."

"I told you the Big Kids would get us."

I nodded. But there were more important worries to distract me. I was pretty sure I knew the way out, but the chamber around us didn't seem familiar. I started tracing the way back, trying to remember the path we'd taken.

"You sure this is how we came?" Stu asked.

"I don't know." I didn't recognize the shaft we were in. It led up at a slight angle, but it kept getting narrower. The ceiling was so low, I was almost crawling.

"This can't be right," Stu said.

"Yeah. Maybe we should turn back." I looked ahead. "Hang on—I think it gets wider." Sure enough, a bit farther along the shaft got bigger. Then it opened into a large chamber.

And there were Big Kids there.

Different Big Kids.

I didn't see them at first. I climbed up on a boulder that was near the opening. It was warm. It moved. It wasn't a boulder. It was a toe. A big toe . . .

Stu made a gurgling sound as he stared at the huge foot. To be fair, I wasn't saying much either. In fact, I'm sure any bat in the cave would have had no trouble flying into my open mouth at that moment.

"Hi," one of the Big Kids said. His voice rumbled through the chamber. I looked up. Trickles of light filtered in from cracks in one of the side walls, but the speaker's head was lost in the darkness far above me.

"Uh . . . hi," I said.

"Whatcha doing?" another voice asked.

"We were running from some Big . . . uh, from some bullies," I told him.

"I hate bullies," the first Big Kid said.

"Me, too," another agreed.

"So do I."

I was surprised by this last voice. It was Stu. I

guess once you face your worst fears, you can either crumple up or you can deal with things. To my surprise, Stu seemed to be dealing with the situation. "If you tell me how to get out of here," he said, "I'll bring some tiny little bullies for you to play with. Okay?"

"Deal," one of the Big Kids said. A huge hand descended from the darkness and reached out to seal the bargain with a shake. Stu held out his own insignificant, microscopic hand and grasped the Big Kid's fingertip.

"Go straight back until you reach the wall," the Big Kid said. "Then keep making lefts. You can't miss the exit."

"Thanks." Stu headed out.

I started to follow him, but he turned and said, "Stay here. This is for me to do."

He went off, walking tall, then ducked into the tunnel and disappeared. I stayed and made small talk with the Big Kids. I wasn't sure what they were like, and I didn't want to say anything that might upset them, so I let them do most of the talking. In a while, I heard the sounds of a mob heading this way. Stu came racing in, panting and puffing but looking pretty happy to be in the lead.

"Get the little weasel!" someone behind him shouted.

"Smash him!"

"Pound him to bits!"

They came tearing in after Stu, popping one by

one through the narrow opening like marbles spilling out of a bottle.

Hands swept down and grabbed the bullies the way I'd grab a root beer from the cooler in the corner store. The hands rose again, with tiny arms and legs dangling at all angles, kicking and twitching and flailing. There were some shouts and a lot of whimpers.

"Thanks, guys," Stu said as we walked to the exit of the chamber.

"Our pleasure," a Big Kid said. He rattled a bully in his fist like a can of spray paint that needed mixing. "Thanks for the toys. Come see us again."

"We sure will," Stu said. He led us out.

"What do you feel like doing?" I asked as we walked away from the mouth of the cave. It was still early.

"I don't know," Stu said.

"How about the dump?" I suggested.

Stu's face creased with a frown. "But there might be . . ." He stopped, and the frown faded. Then he smiled. "Sure," he said. "Let's go."

# YOUR WORST NIGHTMARE

It's over. The nightmare is over. Just in time. I couldn't run much farther. I could hardly breathe. Larry looked even worse. But we didn't have to run. I'd saved us. My idea worked. I could stand here now and catch my breath and wonder how things had gotten so quickly out of hand.

I probably shouldn't have been hanging out with Larry in the first place. He can be a really big jerk. But I'm not too good at making friends, so I didn't have a lot of choices. I usually ended up spending my free time with Larry. Mostly, I didn't get involved when he was being a jerk. I didn't try to stop him, but I didn't take part.

But the Clayton kid blamed both of us. It was

all Larry's doing. That didn't matter. We both got blamed.

I don't know where Larry got the phrase— probably from some movie. That's how it started with the Clayton kid. What was his name? Ricky. That was it—Ricky Clayton. He's this real quiet kid who doesn't ever bother anyone or do anything much at all. Even so, there's something spooky about him.

But mostly I guess he was in the wrong place at the wrong time. He was walking down the street toward Larry when Larry was in that mean mood of his.

"Hey, what are you looking at?" Larry said as the kid got close to him.

"Nothing," the kid mumbled. I guess he didn't realize what a dangerous answer that was.

"Nothing? You calling me nothing?" That's when Larry grabbed the kid by the shirt. Larry really liked to do that. He'd grab a handful of cloth and buttons, right below the neck, and then twist his fist. I think he'd gotten that from a movie, too.

"Come on, leave me alone." The kid squirmed a bit but didn't try to break loose.

"You know what I am?" Larry asked him. I could tell he was getting ready to use the phrase.

The kid shook his head.

*"You know what I am?"* Larry yelled, putting his face right up close so his nose was almost in the kid's eye.

"No . . ."

"I'm your worst nightmare." Larry gave the kid a push.

The kid stumbled backward and fell down hard on his butt. I expected him to start crying, or to turn and run. He wasn't very big. Larry would never do something like that to anyone who had a chance of fighting back. But the kid didn't cry or run. Instead he stared at Larry and said, "You don't know anything about nightmares."

I guess that took Larry by surprise. He didn't say a word. Then the kid spoke again. "But you will. Real soon." He stood up slowly, his eyes still locked on us. "Your worst nightmare is coming. It's on its way."

"You're crazy," Larry said. He shook his head. "Let's get out of here. This kid has lost his mind."

I didn't need much convincing. The Clayton kid was far too strange. We walked away. Behind us, I heard the kid say, "For both of you."

As we went down Lincoln Street, the breeze picked up. The air filled with whirling maple seeds that had been blown down from three trees that grew in the yard of a house near the corner.

Whenever I saw Larry rough up someone, I found myself acting extra friendly afterward, sort of wanting to make sure he still liked me. Maybe that's why I started to tell him my deep secret. "Hey, you ever pretend that those seeds are—"

"What was that?" Larry said, pointing in front of us.

I didn't see anything. "Where?"

He shook his head. "Nothing. Let's go this way." He turned down Spring Street.

"Sure." I followed and thought about spilling my secret. But Larry had other things to talk about.

"Did you see that kid's face when I pushed him?" he asked, grinning. He opened his eyes wide, imitating the kid, then snorted in amusement.

"Yeah, he really looked surprised," I said.

"*Bam*, right down on his butt," Larry said. "That'll teach him to show me some respect."

"You got that right," I said.

We'd gone less than a block when Larry stopped again. This time he just stood there and pointed.

This time, I saw it.

He must have been close to seven feet tall. He might have been alive once. Imagine a man made inside out. Give him claws. Give him fangs and an attitude. Now imagine something twice as awful. That's what stood in front of us. If he caught up with us, I think we'd get torn to pieces quicker than you could let out a scream. From the muscles that rippled on the outside of his arms, I know he could pull us apart as easily as a couple of wet napkins.

Larry turned and ran down Spring, crossing Lincoln. I stuck right with him.

"What was that?" I managed to ask as we ran.

"My nightmare," Larry told me. "My worst nightmare."

"Oh man. You dream that kind of stuff?"

Before Larry could answer, we had to stop. The monster from his nightmare was in front of us, at the corner of Spring and Hickory.

This time, he was closer.

Just like in a nightmare.

We cut down Spring Street. "Let's go to one of the houses," I said. "Let's get inside."

"No. I do that sometimes in the nightmare. Then I'm trapped."

"Do you ever get away?" I asked.

Larry shook his head. "He always catches me."

We ran. He chased us, but he always ended up ahead of us. "We're dead," Larry gasped. He was panting so hard he was spraying spit with each breath. "That kid. He did this."

I thought about the kid. As we'd left, he'd said, "For both of you." For Larry for what he'd done, and for me for standing there and letting it happen. The very thought of my worst nightmare coming to life made my guts churn. But maybe two bad things could cancel each other out.

"This way," I said, heading back toward Lincoln.

Larry followed. He was starting to moan softly each time he breathed. I think he was running out of strength. "Sometimes, I find a gun," Larry said, gasping between sentences. "I shoot it, but it keeps coming."

"This time is different," I said.

We made it to Lincoln. We had to keep changing direction on the way. But we made it. I stopped before we reached the maple trees. "We can rest here," I told Larry. "We're safe."

"What . . . ?" That was all Larry could get out.

"That's my worst nightmare," I said, looking at the trees.

"Huh?" Then Larry pointed toward the corner. "Got to run." His nightmare stood ahead of us, at the other side of the maples.

"No. Let him come."

I waited. I think Larry still wanted to run, but he couldn't find the strength. I watched the seeds whirling down, imagining what would happen if they suddenly became as sharp as razors.

A stray seed whirled at me, caught by a gust of wind. The seed glanced off my forehead. I could feel something warm and wet running down my face. Blood. In front of us, Larry's nightmare slowly lurched forward. But it was almost over. Larry's worst nightmare was about to walk right through my own worst nightmare.

"We're okay," I said.

"You're bleeding."

I shook my head. "Doesn't matter." I held my breath for a moment as Larry's nightmare tried to pass through the cloud of swirling seeds. It was like watching tomatoes in a blender. I had to turn away. I looked at Larry's face. He was staring straight ahead, watching his nightmare get shredded.

"My nightmare . . ." He still hadn't caught his breath.

"It's okay," I said. "It's over."

"My nightmare," he said again. He kept staring. I didn't know how he could stand to look at that mess. "Sometimes, I find an ax." He took a small step backward.

"It's over," I said. I risked a peek beneath the maples. Larry's nightmare was now thousands of scattered shreds.

"I use the ax. I chop my nightmare to pieces." He took another step back. Then he grabbed my shirt and twisted it and put his face an inch from mine. "It doesn't matter. The pieces just keep coming."

I looked past Larry to the spot where his nightmare should have ended.

"No," I gasped as my blood froze in my veins and my muscles fell slack from fear. "No . . ."

Larry was right. The pieces were coming. They were small. But they were fast. Suddenly, the maple seeds didn't seem all that awful. Suddenly, I had a new worst nightmare. I tried to run, but the pieces were everywhere.

# PHONE AHEAD

**N**ormally, Joe wouldn't pick through garbage, but he'd glimpsed the edge of a shiny plastic case in the trash basket on the corner of Watson Street. *Electronics,* he thought as he leaned over and reached inside. Oh yes. Whatever it was, it certainly wasn't trash. *Who would throw out a cellular phone?* Joe wondered as he pulled the object from its nest of crumpled papers and crushed cans.

"Probably doesn't work," he said to himself as he flicked the on/off switch and held the phone to his ear. That's when he got his first surprise of the day. He heard someone talking. Joe listened for a moment, then said, "Hello? Hey, I found this phone. Can you hear me?"

But the voice on the other end didn't respond to him. The man was speaking to someone else. "I just saw it on the news," the man said.

"Lucky everybody got out," a woman said. "Can you imagine what would have happened if there were lots of people in the bus station when the fire started? That would have been terrible."

*The bus station?* Joe thought. He hadn't heard anything about a fire, and he hadn't heard any sirens. But if the man just saw it on the news, it might still be happening. Joe had to go see. He switched off the phone and slipped it in his pocket. Then he jogged to the bus terminal.

"They must be crazy," he said when he reached the station. There was no sign of a fire. Joe looked at the clock on the bank across the street. It was seventy-four degrees. It was ten in the morning. He went home and put the phone in his desk drawer.

That evening, Joe was walking through the living room as his parents watched the news. "A fire broke out at the bus station around five this evening," the announcer reported.

Joe couldn't believe it. He listened to the rest of the story, trying to compare the details to what he had heard on the phone.

"No one was hurt, but the station was badly damaged. We'll have more information on the eleven o'clock report."

A shiver ran down Joe's back, then twisted through his stomach. He rushed to his room and grabbed the phone. He switched it on, but all he got was dead silence.

He tried the phone again an hour later. The line was still dead. But on the next try, right before he went to bed, Joe heard the two people talking again.

"I just hate this weather," the man said.

Joe looked out the window. Stars twinkled in a cloudless sky.

"I don't mind the rain," the woman said, "but ever since I was a kid I hated thunder."

Joe could hear a crackle over the line like there was lightning in the air. *Definitely crazy,* he thought as he turned off the phone and went to sleep.

Six hours later, clouds filled the night sky. A heavy rain fell. The first thunderclap woke Joe. Lightning danced across the clouds in jagged flashes. *Maybe they aren't crazy,* Joe thought as he watched the storm.

Joe started checking the phone as often as he could. Whatever the man and woman talked about—the weather, the news, the latest episode of their favorite television show—happened just as they said. But each event took less time to come true than the last. The future Joe overheard in the phone kept getting closer to the present. But none of it was worth anything to him.

The next day, Joe finally heard something exciting.

"Imagine that," the man said. "All those bags of money lying there—right on Adams Street, just past the corner at Main."

"Can you believe it was there for over an hour before the police found it?" the woman asked. "The robbers must have dropped the loot when they were getting away. Good thing Adams isn't a busy street. It's still pretty amazing nobody picked up the money."

Joe switched off the phone. This was better than knowing the weather or the news. This was information he could use. Main and Adams streets were less than half a mile away. Joe started running. He reached Main and headed toward Adams. As he turned the corner, he saw bulging canvas bags scattered across one side of the street.

Joe ran down the block, his eyes fixed on the sacks. A police car came speeding past. It slid to a stop right next to the money. Two officers jumped out, grabbed the sacks, and tossed them into the trunk.

"Stupid phone," Joe said as he watched the patrol car drive away. He was so frustrated he almost threw it in the garbage. What good was knowing the future, he asked himself, if he couldn't get there in time?

Joe started walking home, holding the phone in his hand. He kept wondering what the man and woman were discussing right now. Probably chatting about the weather, he thought. Or something stupid, like a new movie. But maybe it was something *really* important . . .

Joe felt like he was holding onto the last piece of popcorn from a box. He couldn't leave it untasted.

He had to try again. As he started across Bridge Street, he switched on the phone. *Tell me something I can use,* he thought. *That's all I want. Tell me something important. Just one small thing.*

He held the phone to his ear. They were talking. Joe relaxed. Hearing the voices was like running into old friends.

"Poor kid," the woman was saying.

There was a sadness in the woman's tone that caused Joe to stop walking and listen carefully.

"Yeah, I saw it on the news. It's a shame he died."

Joe shook his head. "Who cares," he muttered. This didn't sound like anything useful or important. But he kept the phone to his ear. He couldn't help himself.

"He was just standing there," the man said, "right in the middle of Bridge Street, by the place where the road curves. Imagine that. I wonder what was on his mind? They say he didn't even see the truck."

*Truck?* Joe thought as he heard the blare of a horn and the shriek of large tires skidding around the curve behind him. *What truck?*

"Cool," Lisa said as she looked down into the garbage can next to a lamppost on Bridge Street. She reached inside, wondering why someone would throw away a cellular phone. "Probably doesn't even work," she said. She switched it on and held it to her ear. She smiled as she heard voices. This, she thought, could be very interesting.

# SAND SHARKS

**K**elly had the sand castle almost perfect when Michael ran across the beach, screaming like a wild man. He smashed right through her marvelous castle, blowing it into fine fragments of sand that fell in a shower around her.

"Michael!"

"Sorry," he said, barely glancing over his shoulder. "Didn't see it."

"Yes you did. You ruined it on purpose."

Michael turned toward Kelly and shook his head. "Didn't," he said in a calm voice.

"Did!" Kelly shouted.

"Kids," Dad said, looking up from his magazine. "Stop fighting. This is supposed to be a vacation.

Kelly, you're old enough to know how to behave. You should set an example for Michael."

"But Michael ruined my castle," Kelly said. "And he did it on purpose. Just like he ruins everything."

Mom glanced up from her book. "I'm sure it was an accident. There's no need for all this shouting." She shifted her eyes back to her reading before Kelly could answer.

Kelly looked at Michael. Michael looked back, grinning. Then, as if to make sure she knew it was no accident at all, he stuck out his tongue.

Kelly grabbed a fistful of sand, squeezing it so hard she could almost imagine it forming into a hunk of rock. It would feel wonderful to hurl it at Michael. That would knock a little manners into him. Her arm tensed.

"Listen, kids," Dad said, "your mom and I want to go back to the hotel and pick up some lunch for everyone. Can we trust the two of you to stay here alone?"

"Sure," Michael said. "No problem."

Kelly let the sand trickle from her fingers. *Alone out here?* The place was so bare and empty. They were the only people on the beach, and there weren't a whole lot of people on the island. A dozen frightening thoughts flashed through Kelly's mind.

"Well, Kell?" her Dad asked.

"Better take her with you," Michael said. "She's scared."

"Am not," Kelly said. She looked at her dad. "Sure, we'll be fine." The words fell from her mouth like specks of foam at the edge of a wave. In an instant, they were lost on the beach.

"Stay out of the water," Mom said. "We'll hurry back."

Kelly watched her parents walk up the beach to the road and wedge themselves into the small rental car. In a moment, the car was puttering along the narrow pathway. In another moment, it was out of sight.

Michael headed right for the ocean.

"Hey," Kelly said, "they told us not to."

"They aren't here, are they?" Michael walked deeper, kicking up water with each step.

Kelly glared at him. *I hope you drown,* she thought. Instantly, she felt awful for making such a terrible wish.

Michael screamed.

Kelly's heart slammed against her chest. Her brother slashed his arms down, striking at something in the water. He screamed again. Then he lurched and disappeared beneath the water.

"Michael!" Kelly ran to the edge of the ocean. She searched for any sign of her brother. She rushed into the water, unsure of what to do. "Mom! Dad! Come back! Help!" Kelly yelled toward the road. It was useless. They were gone. She ran farther out. The surf lapped at her knees. "Michael, where are you?" she called, desperately scanning the ocean.

Suddenly the water next to her exploded. A huge shape shot up from the ocean in a spray of white foam. Kelly jumped back, scraping her heel on a jagged shell. The thrashing creature next to her roared.

Then it laughed.

"That's not funny!" Kelly shouted.

"You should have seen your face." Michael laughed again as he walked back toward the sand. He left the water and plunked down on a towel.

Kelly felt trapped. She knew she wasn't supposed to be in the water, but she didn't want to join her brother. It was always that way—Michael broke the rules, and then she got in trouble.

Kelly wanted to get even. There had to be some way. Maybe she could scare him.

"Watch out for the sand sharks," she called.

"What?"

"Sand sharks," she repeated. "They'll get you."

"Don't be stupid," Michael said. "Sand sharks live in the water."

"Nope," Kelly told him. "Not around here. Around here, they live in the sand. And they hunt for boys. I read about them in the guidebook."

"Yeah, right." Michael sprawled across the beach towel.

Kelly remained in the water. She watched Michael, wondering what he would do next. She was sure he wasn't through ruining her day. He had one foot in the sand by the corner of the towel, digging in with his toes. Suddenly he jerked his leg and stuck his foot deeper.

"Help!" he screamed.

Kelly wasn't amused.

"Ow! Help!" Michael twisted around like a fish on a hook. He thrust his foot farther into the sand. "Kelly, help me!"

"Yeah, right," she said, repeating the words he'd used a moment earlier. She wasn't going to fall for his tricks twice in one day. "You'll have to do better than that."

Somehow, Michael dug his foot even deeper in the sand. Kelly was amazed that her brother would work so hard to scare her.

"Ahhhh!" He was making fake screams now, not even shouting real words. He was really flopping around. He thrashed his arms and kicked at the sand with his other foot. Then he stuck that one in, too.

Kelly wondered how long he would keep it up. He'd actually gotten his legs into the sand all the way up to the knees. She hadn't thought that would be possible. It sure looked uncomfortable. Still, it was all wasted effort. She'd never fall for such a ridiculous trick.

Twisting and wriggling, Michael managed to get buried all the way up to the top of his bathing suit. "Kelly," he said weakly.

Kelly had an idea. She decided to play along just enough to make him think she was fooled.

After all, the sand shark story was her idea to begin with. "Oh, all right, I'll help you." She walked slowly toward the shore. But she promised herself she wouldn't run or scream when he leaped up and shouted. She'd just laugh at him. It would be perfect.

Kelly waded through the surf, taking small steps to make Michael wait. She enjoyed the way the water felt as it ran back to the sea, tickling her toes. Her brother was still making sounds, but they made no sense. She braced herself, knowing he would jump up and shout "Boo!" when she got close.

He didn't.

By the time Kelly reached Michael, all she could see was the top of his head. A moment later, the sand closed in over that, leaving nothing but a tiny crater.

Kelly heard a car coming down the road toward the beach. After the engine stopped, she heard car doors slamming.

"Where's Michael?" Mom called.

"He didn't feel like lunch," Kelly said as she smoothed out the shallow crater with her foot. She decided that after she ate she'd go back into the water as soon as Mom let her. She really didn't want to spend much time on the sand.

# ON THE ROAD

**K**ent spotted a license plate from Alabama. "That makes forty-nine," he said to no one in particular. He'd seen plates from every state except Hawaii.

"That's nice, dear," his mom said from the front seat.

*Now what?* He looked around, trying to find something to help with the numbing boredom of riding in the backseat on a long family trip. A sign on the side of the road told him they were on STATE HIGHWAY 50 WEST. The information didn't mean anything to Kent. The road numbers were hard to keep track of. That was something for parents to worry about.

"Will we be there soon?" Kent asked.

"Not much longer," his dad said.

Kent sorted through the magazines strewn across the seat next to him. He was sure he'd read them all. *How long had they been driving today?* He couldn't even remember what time they had started. It seemed like days ago.

He picked up one of the magazines and thumbed through the worn pages, looking for anything he hadn't read yet. No luck. He tried another. Finally, in the third magazine, he found a page of ads he'd skipped before. That held him for a few minutes.

"Mom, I'm bored," Kent said when he finished reading.

"Why don't you see if you can find a license plate from every state," she suggested.

"I just did that."

"How about something that starts with each letter of the alphabet? Look for something that begins with 'a,' then with 'b,' and so on. That should help you pass the time for a while."

"Okay." Kent glanced out the window to his left. There were plenty of automobiles in sight. That took care of "a." A car passed them in the fast lane. There were two kids in the backseat. A boy a couple years younger than Kent was staring out the side window, his eyes filled with emptiness. Kent looked back. The car sped past them.

"B" for "boy," he realized. And "c" for car.

On the right, a sign read: ALTERNATE ROUTE 37. It meant no more to Kent than any of the other signs. He looked around for something that started with "d."

By the time he reached the letter "m," Kent had grown tired of the game. According to the sign up ahead, they were on an interstate highway now. He felt that he'd been traveling forever. "Dad, will we be there soon?"

"Pretty soon, now," his dad said.

"How long?" he asked. "I mean, in minutes. How many minutes?"

"Don't bother your father while he's driving," his mom said.

"But . . ." Kent let it drop. He leaned forward and looked at the dashboard. The clock needed to be set. It just kept flashing 12:00, over and over, never changing.

He tried to think back to the beginning of the day. He remembered spotting license plates. He remembered doing something before that. What was it? The game. That was it. He'd been playing a handheld video game. But the batteries had died. And before that . . . ? Kent couldn't remember.

He couldn't remember the last time they had stopped to eat. He couldn't remember the last time he had gone to the bathroom. But he wasn't hungry. And he didn't have to go.

*Where are we headed?* He couldn't even remember that. He realized he didn't even know if they were *going* somewhere or *coming back*. He tried to think of other trips. There'd been trips every year. There'd been short trips when they'd just driven a few miles to visit some friend of his parents. There'd been longer trips when they went on vacation. Each year, it seemed to take a bit longer. They traveled a bit farther. They spent a bit more time in the car.

*How long had they been on this road?* Kent looked at the passing signs, hoping for any hint of his location. There was nothing on the road ahead. "Where are we?" he asked.

"Getting there," his father said.

"Be patient," his mother said.

Kent sighed.

It started to rain, putting a fine mist on the windshield. His father switched on the wipers. Kent looked at the dashboard again. He looked at the fuel gauge. It showed slightly less than half a tank. He tried to remember the last time he had looked at it. They hadn't stopped for gas in a long time. At least, he couldn't remember the last time they'd filled the tank.

"I need batteries for my game," Kent said.

There was silence from the front seat. He wondered if his mom was angry. Finally she said, "Maybe next time we stop. You'll have to wait. Just take a nap now or something."

Kent took a nap. He woke. They were on the road. The clock flashed 12:00. The gas gauge was just below half a tank. The batteries in his game were dead. The seat next to him was covered with magazines he'd already read.

He looked out the window. There was a car with a license plate from Kentucky. Maybe he could find all the states—except Hawaii. That would help pass the time.

"There's Oklahoma," Kent announced. He saw a car from Pennsylvania next. *That's two,* he thought. This wouldn't take long at all. But at least the game would kill a little time.

Sooner or later, Kent knew, they had to get there. No trip could last forever, could it?

# THE LANGUAGES OF BEASTS

**M**ornings started out fine. Diana liked the beginning of the day, with birdsongs waking her as the whistled notes floated through her open window. She'd always lie in bed for a few minutes, just listening to the music, holding onto the pleasure until her mother's grating voice called her down for breakfast.

*Why couldn't people sound like birds?* Diana wondered. Or better yet, why couldn't people be silent?

Luckily her mother didn't talk much, and the birdsongs could be heard in the kitchen, so breakfast wasn't bad. The walk to school was nice. At least, the first part always gave her pleasure. Diana left the house and looked both ways, hoping to see one of the neighborhood cats. She smiled as she spotted Ragtag. He lived next door but always ran up for petting when Diana called him.

"Here, Ragtag."

The cat, lying sprawled in the morning sun, rolled to his paws and padded over. He rubbed his head against Diana's leg and purred loudly. Diana spent a minute with Ragtag, then resumed her walk to school. After another block, she paused to say hi to her next friend.

"Good morning," she said to the dog. She didn't know his name, but he was almost always there, straining at the limit of a long rope in the front yard, wagging his tail and barking.

And that was about the end of the good part of the morning. The next few blocks brought her into the crowded place, filled with people who jabbered and talked about stupid things. Diana wished there were fewer people. Wherever she looked, she saw unpleasant sights. There was a man eating a doughnut while he walked to work. Didn't he realize how revolting he looked, cramming food in his mouth, bending halfway over in an attempt to avoid getting powdered sugar on his suit? Diana shook her head and snickered at the sight. And the two women ahead of her— Diana couldn't believe how silly their conversation was. All they talked about was the television shows they'd watched the night before.

By the time she reached her school, Diana was in a crowd of chattering kids. She tried to ignore them. They were all so silly. There was Annie, who jabbered on and on about shopping. And there was Billy the Blabbermouth, who talked about nothing but baseball. Diana couldn't stand the kids in her class. They almost never said anything to her, and when they did it was something mean and cruel But she didn't care—they were just stupid kids with nothing important to say.

The school day was miserable—it never failed to amaze her how uninteresting her teachers were—but Diana had something to look forward to. The end of the school day was not far away. Diana knew her walk home would bring her back to the animals.

When the last bell rang, Diana dashed from the school. On the way out, a redheaded girl from her neighborhood caught her eye.

"Hi," the other girl said.

Diana ignored her. She knew the girl just wanted to taunt her or make fun of her. She hurried through the crowded section of town. At the corner by the doughnut shop, she waited impatiently for the light to turn green. Around her, people talked, saying words that meant nothing.

The light changed.

As Diana was about to step from the curb, a woman cut right in front of her. Diana stumbled as she tried to avoid running into the woman.

*How rude,* Diana thought. Before she knew what she was doing, she reached out and grabbed the woman by the shoulder. She wanted to tell her to watch where she was going.

The woman stopped dead as Diana touched her.

A horn blasted at Diana. A car shot past them, running the light, just missing the woman.

Diana stood with her mouth open.

"You saved me," the woman said. "You saved my life." She reached toward Diana with her right hand.

Diana wanted to pull away. She wanted to escape the touch. She couldn't. She was locked in place, facing this woman, stuck to her spot as the crowds moved past like water flowing around two rocks in a stream.

"Your deepest wish," the woman said, brushing a fingertip across Diana's forehead. The finger felt dry and sharp. "What is your wish?"

At that moment, nothing else existed in the world. All Diana saw or knew was herself, the woman, and the power to have her deepest wish. Whatever she wanted—it would be hers. She knew. She believed. The words came by themselves. "The animals," she said.

The woman smiled. "Tell me—exactly."

"Their speech," Diana said, growing bolder as she heard her own words. "I want to understand them." She knew that this alone of all things would make each day of her life a joy. She would not just hear the songs and purrs and barks but would know the languages. The thought of such a talent nearly caused her to burst with anticipation. "Can you give me that?"

The woman brushed Diana's forehead again, very gently. "It is done."

The woman drifted away with the passing people.

For an instant, Diana's brain felt as if it held the heat of a thousand suns. Just as quickly, the feeling vanished. Diana was transfixed by the strangeness of the moment. The traffic light changed. It changed again. Pedestrians moved around her, talking, pushing. Diana smiled. She was sure she had the gift. She took a step. She walked, then she ran, moving away from the crowds of jabbering humans, rushing toward the animals who were her friends.

She hoped to see *him*. It would be so perfect if he was the first to speak to her. Yes. Diana trembled with wonder and expectation. There he was, a block away. He strained against the end of his leash at the edge of the lawn as she approached. "Hi, doggie," Diana said.

He barked.

"Stupid animal," he said. "Walking on two legs. How ugly and stupid. You don't even have a tail to wag."

Diana pulled her hand back. She rushed down the street, unwilling to believe the cruel words she'd heard. She stopped to catch her breath. There had to be some kind of mistake—some misunderstanding.

"You smell."

Diana looked down. Ragtag was at her feet, purring.

"You awful, stinky creature," the cat said,

rubbing its head against her leg. "Even my scent can't cover your smell."

Diana ran home. Above her head, the birds called to one another.

"Look, there's that silly one with the big head."

"Watch me get her."

Something splattered on the sidewalk next to Diana as she ran.

"Look at her, can't even fly."

"Can't sing, either. Just jabber, jabber, jabber."

"Imagine going around on those thick legs."

"She sure is stupid."

Diana ran inside and slammed her door. The birdsong came through the open windows.

"Humans are so useless."

"They ruin everything."

Diana forced the window shut. She ran to her room and sat on her bed, huddling in the corner.

Quiet. It was finally quiet.

Until the whisper. "Oh no, she's back."

Another whisper. "I hate it when she's here."

"I wish we could make a giant web and be rid of them."

Diana lifted her chin from her knees and stared at the ceiling.

"What are you looking at?" the spider asked.

Across the room, an ant laughed.

Beneath the bed, a thousand tiny insects shouted at her and called her terrible names. "Worm meat!" "Stink creature!" "Sack of flesh!"

Night fell. The crickets joined in.

# CLASS TRIP

'd really been looking forward to our class trip. I know I'd gone there before, but I can't get enough of the Center City Science Museum. I could tell that the rest of the kids were ready, too. Everyone was full of energy when we walked into class.

That's when I saw him. "Oh no," I groaned, "not Mr. Peggler."

"Phooey," Dale said. He curled his nose and sniffed like he'd smelled something bad.

You'd think a classy private school like Wolfson Academy could afford to hire good substitutes. And, to be honest, I guess I'd have to say that most of the time they did. But Mr. Peggler was terrible. He thought he was great with kids, but he had no idea what we really liked.

*This is going to ruin the trip,* I thought. I'd been looking forward to going to the museum with Ms. Howell. She was such a great teacher.

"Listen up," Mr. Peggler said. "Your teacher is out today. But don't worry, we're still going on the class trip. Isn't that wonderful?"

There was silence in the room.

"Well," Mr. Peggler said, "I'm looking forward to it. So, let's go get on that bus and have a great time."

We got on the bus. I took a nap. Morning isn't my best part of the day. When we reached the museum, Mr. Peggler led us into the lobby.

"We always go to the Hall of Mammals," I told him. "That's our favorite place." I loved seeing the bunnies and the squirrels and the other small creatures.

"Well," he said, looking around at the signs on the wall, "it's no good to get into a rut. You need to experience new things. Otherwise you'll all become creatures of habit. Ah, this is perfect," he said, pointing to one of the signs. "There's a show about to start in the planetarium."

I shook my head. "I don't think that's such a good idea."

"It's a wonderful idea," he said.

Then I saw the name of the show and a chill ran across my scalp. "I *really* don't think it's a good idea at all."

"What's wrong, afraid of the dark?" Mr. Peggler asked.

"Hardly," I said.

Before I could argue any further, he was leading everyone into the planetarium. We took our seats. The room grew dark. Mr. Peggler was sitting right next to me. "See," he said as the stars appeared projected on the ceiling. "This is wonderful. You should just relax and enjoy the show."

"Welcome to the planetarium," the taped voice of the announcer said over the loudspeaker.

"I really think we should leave," I told Mr. Peggler.

He shushed me. Okay, I thought. That's it. I'd tried. There was nothing more I could do except sit and listen to the announcer.

"Our show is called *Phases of the Moon*. If you look toward the eastern horizon, you'll see a spectacular full moon rising."

It was a fake, of course. I wasn't really sure if it would work. But it certainly did the trick. By the time the whole moon was visible over the horizon, we'd all changed. I'd tried to tell Mr. Peggler it was a bad idea taking us to the planetarium. Maybe I should have told him our secret. But what use is a secret if it gets out? And even if I'd told him we were all werewolves, he'd never have believed me. But it's true. When the full moon rises, we turn into wolves. All of us. I don't mean those pretty wolves you see in nature shows on TV—I mean snarling, raging, howling monsters.

The school should have known better than to hire him. I guess good substitutes are hard to find. Of course, by the time we get through with Mr. Peggler, he's going to be pretty hard to find, too.

# COLLARED

Jay was always getting me into trouble. I mean, I got myself into trouble, but I got there by following Jay. Still, the fact that he would hang around with a younger kid like me was enough to make up for the occasional problem with parents, teachers, or other adults. It's not that we ever did anything really bad, it's just that whatever we did seemed to end up causing some kind of problem.

So, on Friday night when I met him in town, I figured nothing he suggested would surprise me.

I was wrong.

"Hey, Marty," he said when I walked up to him. He was leaning against the office building on the corner of Stoker and Main, looking tough and cool in his black leather jacket. No matter what the weather, hot or cold, Jay wore that jacket. Most of the time, he slicked back his hair, too. It looked kind of strange, sort of like in those old movies where the kids spend all their time dancing or racing their cars. But the last kid who laughed at Jay's hair ended up unable to laugh at anything for a few weeks after that. Jay didn't take disrespect from anyone. That was another nice part of hanging around with him. Nobody gave me any trouble when we were together.

"Jay," I said, giving him a handslap. "What's up?"

"We are," he said. "Up the hill."

"What? You don't mean up there, do you?" I pointed past Jay's shoulder.

He gave me a look that said "You heard right" and started walking toward Varny Street.

I almost didn't follow. *Up the hill.* There was only one meaning for that in our town. And none of us went up the hill. Not up there. Not at night.

But Jay was going.

I was torn. I'd follow Jay almost anywhere. But up the hill? I wasn't sure I could do that. The heels of his boots made a tap-tap that started talking to me. Instead of "tap-tap, tap-tap," I found myself hearing "go back, go back." The sound grew fainter; the voice became a murmur and then a memory as Jay left me behind. I waited for him to look at me. He kept walking.

While my head struggled with the decision, my legs made a choice. I jogged to catch up with him. As we climbed the long hill, I didn't speak, fearing that my voice might reveal my feelings. Varny Street starts out fine. It's lined with houses like any normal street. Then the houses give way to a few empty lots. Then the lots give way to trees. Nobody wants to build a house too close to the top.

Halfway up the hill to *there*, I finally had to say something. "Why?"

Jay turned his head toward me but didn't stop walking. "No reason," he said. Then he laughed. I thought he was done, but a moment later he said, "Maybe because no one else will."

I couldn't believe I was following him up to the old Morgan house. Even if I ignored the stories kids told, there had to be enough real dangers to make anyone with half a brain stay away. I'd bet the place was filled with rats, and the floors were rotting to pieces. I could see myself crashing through the floor, landing in the cellar. I shuddered as I saw my legs snap like toothpicks against the hard concrete. Nobody went near the Morgan house. Even the adults didn't like to walk past it. Most of them sort of whispered the name when they mentioned it at all. It was like a rule in our town—don't talk about the Morgan house.

I don't know the story. It's hard to know the story when nobody will tell it. But I knew it was a bad place. Ahead, I watched Jay. The leather of his jacket flexed as he walked, a deep black patch in the dim light from the streetlamps at the bottom of the hill.

We were almost at the top. The wind gained force, stealing the heat from my body and making me shiver. I tried to tell myself that it was only the cold that made me tremble. Jay pulled up his collar. "Leather," he said. "Nothing like it."

I hoped he wouldn't start on that. There was one area where Jay drove me crazy. He'd talk about leather and how great it was and how wonderful it felt. "It breathes," he'd say, stroking his sleeve. "Keeps you warm without getting too hot. Feels great. There's nothing like it." I just couldn't get excited about it, but I certainly wasn't going to point that out to Jay.

I looked up. We were there. The house, dark, silent, and shut tight, towered above us. Loose shingles jutted from the roof. Most of the windows were broken. All the ones I could see were covered with boards from the inside. I wished the house would collapse before we went in. I hoped it wouldn't collapse after we went in.

Jay hopped the low fence, then looked back at me and grinned. "Coming?"

I crawled over the fence, but I felt like I'd left my stomach on the sidewalk behind me. It almost felt like I'd left my spine there, too, but I managed to follow Jay up the steps to the porch.

"Locked," Jay said as he rattled the knob.

"Guess we can't get in," I said, turning back toward the street. I hadn't even reached the edge of the porch when the sound of a crash ripped through the night, hitting me like a jolt of electricity. I spun back toward Jay.

He was standing half inside the doorway. He'd rammed the old wood of the door with his shoulder. Jay bowed and swept his hand forward. "Shall we?"

"Sure." That word didn't seem to want to leave my throat. I walked into a world that reeked of dust and mildew. I had to fight to keep from coughing.

There was a click. A beam of light splashed through the dark. Jay had brought a flashlight. "Let's explore," he said, walking deeper into the place I didn't want to be.

I followed him into a large room directly beyond the front door. Not wanting to stare into the blind darkness at our sides, I tried to keep my eyes focused on the wedge of floor that was carved by Jay's light. There wasn't as much dust on the floor as I expected. At the edges of the light, I could see heavier layers of dust on the furniture.

We went deeper—through another room and along a short hall that led to a stairway. But Jay didn't go up. Instead, he walked to a door in the wall beneath the stairs. Jay opened the door and leaned inside.

"Boo!"

I jumped a mile. Jay laughed. "Down we go," he said. He headed into the cellar.

I really wanted to leave. I wanted to breathe air

that wasn't heavy with dust. I wanted to stand beneath an open sky. But the rooms behind me were dark and Jay had the light.

The steps groaned beneath my feet. I knew we'd end up in a dusty rat-filled basement—a damp hole that would swallow the two of us.

"Whoa, look at this," Jay said, swinging the beam slowly across from wall to wall.

I froze on the steps.

The place was neat and clean. But that wasn't what stopped me. There was a low block of stone in the middle of the floor. A box lay on the block. I knew right away what it was.

"Let's get out of here," I said, grabbing Jay's arm. The leather of his jacket felt almost alive beneath my fingers.

Jay pulled away from me and moved to the coffin. He walked all the way around it, shining the light over every inch of the polished wooden box. "I'd heard stories," he said.

"Let's go," I said again.

"Look what I have." Jay reached into his pocket. He pulled out an object and held it up for me to see. It was a cross on a chain. Jay laughed. "Just in case. But wait, there's more." He reached inside his coat and pulled out a long wooden stake.

"Jay, you've been watching too many vampire movies."

The rest happened very fast.

There was a muffled thump. The lid of the coffin flew open.

I felt every muscle in my body try to leap up the stairs. But I couldn't move.

A dark shape burst from the coffin, snarling. It hit Jay from the side with such force he was knocked off his feet. The flashlight flew from Jay's hand and bounced along the floor, spinning crazily.

The light swept across them—Jay and the vampire.

They were on the ground, struggling. Jay was pinned facedown. The vampire had his arms around Jay and his head buried in Jay's neck. Jay was screaming.

I took a step back.

The flashlight spun slower. Near my feet, something reflected the passing beam.

The cross.

Jay was trying to hit the vampire. He'd managed to hold onto the stake, but all he could do was stab at the air.

I stepped forward, grabbed the cross, and ran to the struggling figures. I held the cross out, my hands shaking so badly I thought my bones would tear loose from their joints.

I pressed the cross against the side of the vampire's head. The skin that touched my fingers felt old and dry and dead.

There was a hiss of scorched flesh, and the room filled with a dreadful stench. The vampire sprang up, its hands clutched over its face. It stumbled against the open coffin and let out a cry unlike anything I had ever heard. Whether hunger or sorrow or anger, I couldn't tell.

Screaming his own howl, Jay struggled to his knees, the stake still gripped in his hand. He staggered to his feet, then rushed at the vampire and plunged the point into the monster's chest.

I turned my head away, but I heard the sound of the stake, like a shovel slicing into mud. When I looked again, the vampire had fallen back into the box. I ran forward and slammed down the lid, then placed the cross on top. The instant it touched the wood, it was as if a lock had snapped shut on the coffin.

I reached over to help Jay. I was afraid to take my eyes from the lid of the coffin, afraid it would fly open again. I felt leather. I grabbed and pulled and backed off, guiding Jay, leading him away. I found the flashlight with my other hand and we stumbled up the stairs.

Jay was almost all deadweight at first. By the time we reached the front room, he had recovered enough to walk without my help. We made it out of the house.

I never realized how much I loved the smell of the outdoors.

Down the street, the flashlight died. I guess something had been damaged when it fell. But we didn't need it anymore.

"Are you . . . ?" I started to ask. "Did it . . . ?"

Jay felt his neck. Then he swore.

"Did it bite you bad?" I asked. There was no doubt the creature in the basement had been a vampire. The cross, the stake, the coffin—there was no question what we had faced. And I knew that anyone bitten by a vampire would turn into one. I moved a step away from Jay, afraid he might change before my eyes.

"Relax." Jay turned and showed me the damage. His collar, in a flipped up position covering his neck, was ripped and torn. There were two holes in the leather. But I didn't see any blood.

"Just the coat?" I asked.

He nodded. "I love this coat," he said, running his fingers along the wounded section.

"Better it than you," I said.

He didn't reply.

We walked back toward town, pausing to rest on a bench at a bus stop. We were just at the edge of the wooded area. "You know what would have happened if he'd bitten you," I said.

Jay nodded.

"But we made it." I looked back up the hill at the house, still not completely believing what we'd been through, or that we had actually escaped.

"I owe you one," Jay said, touching the tears in his collar.

I didn't answer. I wasn't sure whether he was speaking to me or the coat.

We sat in silence. This was not the time to discuss the things that had happened.

I glanced at Jay. He was running his fingers inside his jacket collar. Suddenly he made a choking sound like he had swallowed something just a bit too big to get down in one piece.

The collar of his jacket rippled for an instant.

Jay must have known. He reached for the zipper. He tried. He really tried to escape. The collar snapped around his neck. The ends of the collar stabbed at his flesh. The zipper pulled tighter. Jay grabbed at his throat and gasped.

I reached out to help him. The flap of his pocket slashed at me, almost cutting my hand.

Courage goes only so deep. I ran.

But there was still some courage in me. I didn't race to the bottom of the hill. I ran for the house and the cross. I hurried through the rooms and down the steps, feeling my way through the basement in total darkness, waiting each instant for the vampire to grab me and hurl me to the floor. My hands met warm softness instead of the hard wood of the coffin. For a moment, I didn't understand. Then, thinking back to the fireplace at home, I knew what I was feeling. It had all become ashes. The vampire and his coffin—everything on the slab of stone had turned to ashes. All but the cross. My hand met the metal buried among the remains. I grabbed the cross and I ran back down the hill.

I was too late.

Jay lay on the ground, unmoving, his face pale and drained. There was a hole on each side of his neck. That tore a hole in my heart. But there was one other part much worse. There was one thing that made me clutch the cold, small cross with all my strength.

Jay's jacket was gone.

Out in the trees, in the woods beyond the bench, something rustled and fluttered.

# WHERE DOES ALL THIS STUFF COME FROM?

Story ideas come from all over, and they come in many different ways. If I cut myself shaving, I usually bleed a story or two. If someone says something unusual, or does something strange, it can give me a plot. At times, it's something very *ordinary* that can inspire a story. Here's a look at the story behind the stories in this collection.

*Fairy in a Jar*

Some ideas pop up out of nowhere. This one came to me in the shower. I was struck by the thought of a kid hunting fireflies and catching a fairy. I got dressed and ran to the computer. The whole story poured out in less than an hour. It was the first really good horror story I ever wrote.

*The Touch*

A friend complained that his daughter lost everything she touched. He suggested I write a story about it. I did, though I don't think the result is what he expected.

*At the Wrist*

I keep an idea file where I put anything that might make a good story. One entry said: a boy loses his father's hand and it comes back to punish him. It came out wonderfully wacky. This is easily my silliest story.

*Crizzles*

No idea where it came from. Must have been something I ate.

*Light as a Feather, Stiff as a Board*

I saw kids playing this game at a picnic. I really wanted something magical to happen. When life doesn't give you what you want, you can write your own ending instead.

*The Evil Tree*

When I wrote the opening sentence, I had no idea where the story was going. I do that a lot. I end up with tons of unused openings, but I also get lots of stories that way. It's sort of like doodling with words.

*Kidzilla*

There's a famous short story by Franz Kafka called "Metamorphosis." It's about a man who turns into a disgusting insect. Someone jokingly suggested I should write about a kid who becomes a cockroach. I thought a lizard would be a lot more fun. I started with the opening sentence, and just followed it wherever it wanted to go.

*Everyone's a Winner*

My daughter and I went wild one day playing skee ball at an amusement park. We ended up winning so many of these little stuffed turtles that we couldn't carry them. They just kept spilling from our clutches. That image was the seed for the story.

*A Little Off the Top*

The setting and discomfort come straight from childhood memories. I really didn't like going to the barber when I was a kid. My wife cuts my hair now.

*The Slide*

True story—I was sitting next to a tube slide when a kid came out. He hit the ground—*plock*—and froze for an instant as if he'd just been dropped into the world. Then he looked around and went running off. Some day I guess I'd better confess to the kid's dad that his son inspired such a gruesome story.

*Big Kids*

This sprang from memories of the fear of Big Kids, combined with a thirst for revenge. Bullies beware—the kid you're messing with today might grow up to be a writer.

*Your Worst Nightmare*

As a game, my daughter used to try to avoid falling maple leaves. Why avoid them? I wondered. The answer that came to mind was wonderfully shivery.

*Phone Ahead*

I got the idea for the phone first, then thought up a story about it.

*Sand Sharks*

I wrote the opening scene with no idea where it would go. But I guess I had sharks on my mind.

*On the Road*

Memories, again. Those trips sure did seem to stretch out.

*The Languages of Beasts*

I had the idea for the ending. I like stories that end with a twist, but it's important to plant little hints and clues along the way. Otherwise you end up with a long joke instead of a short story. Luckily, my editor works very hard to keep that from happening.

*Class Trip*

Another story taken from my idea file. Again, all I really started with was the ending.

*Collared*

I wish I knew where this one came from. I think it's one of my scariest stories. As far as I remember, I just started writing, making it up as I went along.

# ACKNOWLEDGMENTS

Many folks had a hand in the fate of these stories. I'd like to thank Alison, my first reader and best critic. Thanks to Joelle for putting up with constant requests that she drop everything and read my latest effort.

Thanks to Ashley and Carolyn Grayson, Dan Hooker, and Jace Foss for believing in me. Without their efforts, this book would never have happened. Thanks to Jonathan Schmidt for pushing me beyond the spot where I'd settled.

Special thanks to Marilyn Singer for taking time from her own busy writing schedule to help me out and offer many brilliant suggestions.

Thanks to Doug Baldwin, an excellent critic, who was never too busy to read what I thrust upon him. Doug also gets credit for giving me the idea that became "The Touch."

For suggestions and support, thanks to Joan Sprung, Liz Koehler-Pentacoff, Lorraine Stanton, and Fred Fedorko. Thanks to Dian Curtis Regan for sharing her wisdom and making me laugh.

Thanks to Casey Mack and Adrienne Fedorko, two excellent young critics. And to Kelly Gribben, Alisa Loparo, and Kevin Connelly for sharing their opinions. Thanks to Michelle Danish for showing me how to play Light as a Feather.

And thanks to my readers. Without you, these stories are just ink on paper. You bring them to life. Enjoy.